Tsar Alexei II

Could History Be Different?
Could Russia Be Saved?

By J.M. Carns

To The Warm, Kind, Empathetic, Brave

Last Tsesarevich of Russia

Alexei Nikolaevich Romanov

And Those Who Knew and Loved You

May You Forever Rest in Peace

In Honor of Alexei's 120th Birthday

Table of Contents

Author's Prologue

It was March 15th, 1917, and World War I was in full swing. Tsar Nicholas II had gone to the front to take command of the Army. He was now rushing back to Petrograd (now and formerly St. Petersburg) on board the imperial train. Backward Russia was ill-prepared for World War I, bringing much suffering. The country buckled under the demands of the war, and Nicholas had made a long string of disastrous decisions. It became clear that Tsar Nicholas would not be able to make it back to the Alexander Palace where his family resided. There was chaos in the streets. The army was mutinying and joining the protestors. The Duma (Russia's ceremonial legislative body) and elements of the Army decided to force Tsar Nicholas to abdicate, in hope of restoring order.

Russia had moments of possible reform. Nicholas's grandfather Alexander II had freed the serfs. Upon Alexander's assassination in 1881 he was working on the concept of constitutional monarchy. Nicholas and his father Alexander III were by most accounts reactionaries, believing in the autocratic concept that the Tsar ruled alone. Under Russian law the much more popular young Tsesarevich Alexei who had so bravely accompanied his father to the front would become Tsar. Nicholas's reform-minded brother

Michael would be regent under the law, since Alexei was 12 years old. Under Russian law a boy Tsar could not rule until the tender age of sixteen. Nicholas quickly realized he would be separated from his delicate, hemophiliac son. He abdicated to his brother Michael on behalf of himself and Alexei. Technically under Russian law he could not abdicate on behalf of his son, but it was accepted. Michael declined to take the throne unless the Russian people held a popular vote. Within a day over three hundred years of Romanov rule was over.

Nicholas and his family were quickly placed under a gentle house arrest by the new liberal Provisional Government, made up of those who had forced his abdication. On most accounts the once proud Tsar accepted his fate with grace and resignation. To protect the Tsar and his family, Prime Minister Alexander Kerensky eventually moved them to Tobolsk in Siberia, to get them away from the turmoil in the capital. The Provisional Government fell in November 1917 to the Bolshevik Communists. Once the Bolsheviks gained control of the royal family in early April 1918, conditions became gradually harsher. The Royal Family was eventually moved to a house in Ekaterinburg, a Bolshevik stronghold in the Ural Mountains. The Bolsheviks originally planned to put Tsar Nicholas on trial and execute him. As anti-revolutionary forces approached, they decided to execute the entire Royal Family, to prevent them from becoming a symbol for their opponents to rally around.

In the early morning hours of July 17th, 1918, the Royal Family was awoken, escorted to the basement, and told to wait to be moved. The now five-foot-six Alexei, who had injured himself weeks before, and never walked again, had to be carried by his five-foot-seven father. The accounts of what happened in that basement are as chaotic as the quickly formed plan. When chairs were requested for the ill Tsarina Alexandra and Alexei, it is reported that one of the executioners privately sniped, "The heir wants to die in a chair, very well let him have one." While the executioners had been given assigned targets, most aimed for the Tsar, instantly killing him, and soon Tsarina Alexandra. Alexei, three weeks short of his 14th birthday, was in shock, but still alive, sitting petrified in his chair. Alexei had become splattered in his father's blood, as Nicholas had instinctively moved to shield Alexei. The commander came up with his pistol and finished him off close range with two bullets behind the ear. His sisters had jewels that the family had been hiding sewn into their clothes, acting as bulletproof vests. The Bolshevik soldiers bayonetted the girls to death.

Alexei, born August 12th, 1904, after four girls, was originally a relief to his family, but the joy was short lived. It was quickly clear that Alexei was a hemophiliac, a disease he inherited through Alexandra's grandmother, Queen Victoria. Alexei, the only male child, was the center of the family attention and adoration. He was very pampered and spoiled, Nicholas and Alexandra being liberal parents as far as discipline goes. As a young child Nicholas nicknamed him "Alexei the Terrible" for his antics. In one account, as he was playing under the dinner table, he took one of the guests' shoes and proudly showed his trophy to his father. When his father sternly told him to return it, Alexei did with a strawberry in the toe. Alexei suffered greatly through bouts of hemophilia. Only one man seemed to be able to cure them, Grigori Rasputin, who many call the Mad Monk. Rasputin supposedly once said, "The Tsesarevich lives while I am alive." Many attribute the influence Rasputin had on the Tsar and Tsarina to some of the bad choices Nicholas made. But while Alexei had periods of great suffering, when he was well, he lived the relatively normal life of a greatly privileged boy.

As Alexei matured, he became much more contemplative and considerate. In his suffering he had developed a great sense of empathy beyond a normal child of his age. Alexei was known to sympathize with those being disciplined. In one case, it is reported that Alexei would not drop the dismissal of a household staff member until the person was reinstated. As Alexei matured, Nicholas would send Alexei to comfort adults in his court who had suffered a loss. Alexei bravely accompanied his father to the front and would eat black bread with the soldiers. When Alexei was offered more regal fare, he is reported to have said, "It's not what soldiers eat." In Alexei's diary entries and letters, he would show great sympathy for animals hit on the road, or soldiers who had been wounded on the front. But Alexei also had a sense of fun and wit.

Sergei, our fictional narrator for our coming story, shares a lot of similarities with Kolya Derevenko, and Leonid Sednev. Kolya Derevenko, Alexei's best friend, was the son of his doctor. Leonid Sednev was the nephew of his footman. Kolya gave an interview in the 1990s, about 80 years after Alexei's death, he was obviously still very emotionally attached to his childhood friend, the young Tsesarevich. But due to the story being in Sergei's voice, Sergei was ultimately made fictional.

What if the Provisional Government had defied Nicholas and had put this empathetic young Tsesarevich on the throne, against Nicholas's protests? Could history have been different? Could Russia have been saved? Now let's read an alternative version of history as it unfolds before Sergei's eyes.

Author's Note

The prologue is meant as a brief synopsis, to introduce readers to the story, and not as an original piece of research. The facts are either well known or based on original source material in the public domain, attested to in multiple sources. The author owes a special gratitude to the book "Alexei: Russia's Last Tsesarevich - Letters, diaries and writings," by George Hawkins. George Hawkins compiled a collection of Alexei's letters, diaries, and the letters and diaries of those around Alexei about him, and translated them into English. This helped the author to get in the mind of Alexei, and think, what might Alexei do. Most of the original material is in the public domain. The story below is a fictional what if of alternative history, completely in the author's own words. Any historical description can largely be attested to by multiple sources in the public domain. A brief bibliography is provided at the end of sources that helped the author both get into the mind of Alexei and provide more realistic historical detail.

Great care has been taken to largely respect the base characters of the historical figures. But keep in mind, some developments or actions could diverge from history, based on the cascading reactions of putting Alexei on the throne. No disrespect is intended to any historical figure, and certainly most of all not to the kind, gentle Tsesarevich who inspired this story.

Chapter 1

I remember when it all started at the Alexander Palace. Alexei's classroom overlooking the grounds was grand but cozy, and where Alexei usually received his lessons. I was the son of the cook, assigned to be Alexei's playmate, we were both 12 years old. His Swiss tutor Pierre Gilliard was going over Alexei's daily lessons, and if seen I was expected to not be heard. Alexei was seated at the ornate table in his simple olive-green soldier's uniform, with red bars on the shoulders. This is what Alexei usually wore since he stopped wearing the sailor uniforms of his youth. I was in the comfy armchair by the window in my best white Russian shirt, and brown pants, that I usually wore in Alexei's presence. There was a knock on the door, and Mr. Gilliard went to confer with a stern-looking soldier.

Mr. Gilliard, a man about 40, with a dark mustache, had a sound of concern in his voice, turning to Alexei. "Your Father has just abdicated the throne. He no longer wishes to be Tsar. He is now trying to return to the Palace."

Alexei's father, Tsar Nikolai, had been away at the front, and his mom was quarantined with Alexei's sisters. The girls had measles, and the Tsarina was determined her fragile son wouldn't become ill.

Alexei looked at Mr. Gilliard with his typical

contemplative concern, his piercing grayish blue eyes, contrasting with his auburn brown hair, and a wisdom beyond his years, and asked, "Am I going to be Tsar?"

Mr. Gilliard replied, "No, your father out of concern for your welfare has resigned on your behalf as well."

Alexei quipped back, "Then who is going to rule Russia, what will happen to our people?"

Mr. Gilliard shrugged, "I do not know, but your father is coming home, and the family will be together."

Alexei looked off in the distance, apparently lost in his thoughts. At that moment several soldiers burst into the room. An elderly uniformed gentleman was in front with an air of superiority.

Mr. Gilliard indignantly said, "You cannot just burst in on the Tsesarevich like this," but was shoved aside and restrained.

Alexei's eyes widened in a look of shock, but he didn't flinch or look away.

The elderly gentleman bowed to Alexei. "My Tsar, we need you to come with us."

Alexei shot back, "I am not Tsar. What about my family?"

The elderly gentleman, "You are Tsar now your majesty. Your father is under arrest and will remain here with your family. You are coming with us."

Alexei forcefully, "If I am Tsar, then I order you to release my family and let me stay."

The elderly gentleman, "Sorry sir, that is not how it works anymore, the Tsar will no longer have absolute authority, but once you come with us you can discuss this with the new government."

Alexei had a combination of bewilderment yet calm on his handsome face, responding, "I am being kidnapped?"

The man replied, "Call it what you want, but you can come with us on your feet, or be carried, those are my orders sir."

Alexei, "Can Mr. Gilliard come with me?"

Elderly Gentleman, "Not at this point."

Alexei pointed to me, "What about Sergei?"

The elderly gentleman gave me a disinterested look, "Who is he?"

Alexei said back, "He is the son of one of our cooks, I need him to assist me."

The elderly gentleman appeared in a moment of contemplation. "Yes, he can come." He then said to me sternly, "You may accompany Tsar Alexei, but if you do not follow our orders, or interfere in any way, you will be shot."

I was overcome with terror, Alexei had always been good to me, and I wanted to be there for him, but I was also terrified.

Alexei by this time had fully gained his composure, stood up, and walked towards me calmly bracing my hand, "Come on Sergei, it will be okay, if we cooperate, they aren't going to hurt us. I'm now Tsar." Alexei then turned to the elderly gentleman, "We are ready to leave with you now," and we followed him and the soldiers out of the room.

We walked down the stairs and towards the door. The Tsarina Alexandra rapidly approached. People say Alexei took his looks after her, she was supposedly quite a beauty in her youth, but the years of worrying about Alexei's health had taken its toll.

Tsarina, "You cannot take my son, he is just a child, he needs to be with his family."

Alexei quickly turned towards her, "Don't worry Mama, they say I'm Tsar now, we will be okay." Alexei was used to his mom's hysterics during his many bouts of hemophilia.

The Tsarina then turned towards the elderly gentleman, "My husband abdicated on behalf of Alexei as well, so he would not be separated from the family."

The elderly gentleman turned toward the Tsarina, "That is not his decision to make."

Tsarina, "I will be informing my husband immediately when he gets home. You will not get away with this."

Elderly Gentleman, "You do that."

Alexei, "I will call you when I can Mama."

As the elderly gentleman took Alexei by the elbow, we walked out the door and between the grand white columns in front of the palace. The crowds were shouting all kinds of disrespect and slurs towards Alexei's father, and the government, as we were put in the back of a fancy red car, with black leather seating, and a removable top. The elderly gentleman and the driver sat up front, and the soldiers were in surrounding trucks.

I could see the look of mental exhaustion on Alexei's face. Alexei turned to me, "We must put on a brave face for Mama, we don't want her to worry. Thank you for coming with me." He had done such a good job at being brave, but now his eyes were watery, looking like he was about to cry.

I didn't know what to say to him or how to comfort him. I was as bewildered by what was happening as he was. They said he was Tsar but were sure not treating him like one. My role had been to play with Alexei, who was I to express myself to him. Speechless, I put my arm around his back, and put my head on his shoulder, and told him, "Of course."

After a drive through St. Petersburg, we silently walked up the steps of the Old Winter Palace, a brilliant red building, it was so grand, but I had never been in it. Since the assassination of Alexei's great grandfather, the royal family spent their time at the Alexander Palace from where we came. We went through the gates into the courtyard in silence. When we came to the grand but empty dining room covered in gold trim, there was a mid-aged man with a big nose and short brown hair. He sat at the corner of a large dining table in a brown suit. There were two plates which sat roast beef and sauerkraut sandwiches, one in front of the man and one in front of an empty chair at the end of the table. We hadn't had lunch, and I was hungry, but I knew neither of the plates were for me.

The man, "Please sit Alexei, join me."

Alexei slightly blushed taken aback, he wasn't used to being referred to so casually by strangers, but he sat down. Alexei looked at me and said, "Sergei, you can have that chair," pointing to the one across from the man. I was shocked to be invited to sit down with him at what seemed a formal occasion. Alexei then cut his sandwich in half and handed me half. The man looked at me with disinterest then turned to Alexei.

The man, "I am Alexander Kerensky. I am with the new government. You will be Tsar. The peasants need continuity. You will stay here for your safety. If you need anything let me know. I want you to be comfortable here son."

Alexei had that inquisitive look on his face he was so

known for, "Mr. Kerensky, if I am Tsar then how are you in charge?"

Kerensky, "The days of autocracy are over, your father has failed the country, the Duma will run the country. The United Kingdom still has a king, but the Parliament is in charge."

Alexei, with a sense of indignation, "Do not disrespect my father."

Kerensky, "We do not have to discuss your father."

Alexei, "Why are you making me Tsar?"

Kerensky, "As I said, the common people need continuity, and you are the heir to the throne. Your father is no longer acceptable. But you are innocent of the crimes of the past. I am trying to hold the country together. You can help me do that."

Alexei, "Can I see my family?"

Kerensky, "No, as the ruler of Russia you cannot be seen to have corrupting influences around you."

Alexei, his face showing a touch of anger, "Can I have my dog, Joy?"

Kerensky, "Yes, we will fetch him and your things, we want you to be as comfortable as possible, but we must keep you safe, and we must calm this situation."

Alexei, "Thank you, it does not look like I am being given a choice. If my being Tsar will help bring peace, then I will cooperate, but you must promise me one thing. You will keep my family safe. If you will not do that, then do to me what you must."

Kerensky, "Yes, the safety of your family is a top priority."

Kerensky then got up after finishing his sandwich and shook Alexei's hand. Looking sympathetically at Alexei, Kerensky then said to Alexei, "You are so young, I am so sorry you are going through this, but this is nothing compared to what so many out there are suffering."

Alexei took his hand but said not a word. We sat there quietly for several hours, neither of us saying a word in this grand but cold place. We were escorted up to our room. It was a plush opulent room with windows facing the interior courtyard, but a bit cold, not like the warmth of the Alexander Palace. Alexei's brown and white spaniel he so adored was there waiting for him joyfully, and his stuff had been brought in, but nothing for me. Alexei smiled for the first time since before we heard of his dad's abdication, as he sat down and greeted his dog. I felt a sense of relief to see him smile, his smile that always filled me with so much warmth.

Alexei, "Sergei, please unpack my things." I set up the room the best I knew how trying hard to remember Alexei's room at the Alexander Palace. Alexei sat back on the couch looking deep in thought and petted Joy. After a few minutes or so, Alexei then sat down at the table and pulled out the chess set. He looked at me with that smile on his face, "Serg, we might as well make the best of this, let's play." I sat down across the little table from him. He always beat me, but I still enjoyed playing with him and his company. Sitting across from Alexei I felt a wave of contentment come over me. While I felt a slight sense of guilt over the thought, it looked like now I might not have to share Alexei's attention with anyone. I had him all to myself.

Dinner was brought to the room for us, pork cutlets, roast potatoes, and cabbage mushroom soup. Rather plain fare for a Tsar. The guard told Alexei that for our security, we weren't allowed to leave our rooms without permission, but if anything was needed to ask the guard. It was becoming clearer that this lavish bedroom, with a luxurious bathroom on the side, was to become our gilded cage.

After dinner, Alexei changed into his night gown and lay down in the huge bed, as I lay on the couch in my clothes. I could see Alexei looking at me with a sympathetic face, pondering what to do. He then said, "Serg, this bed is too big for just me, put on one of my night gowns, and come to bed."

I was in shock, me, the son of a cook, just didn't sleep in the same bed with royalty. But I didn't turn him down.

"Thank you, thank you so much Alexei," I profusely poured out to him.

Alexei with a look of amusement on his face, "Just knock it off and come to bed."

As I lay down in the same bed with the new Tsar of Russia, Alexei said to me, "You know you are my good friend."

Not knowing what to say back to him. I just said, "Thank you for your kindness."

Alexei amused, "That isn't exactly what you say to a friend, but we'll work on it."

And it dawned on me, the Tsar of Russia wanted me to address him as a friend. Alexei was my best friend, but I had never dared address him in such a fashion. Even though I had been Alexei's playmate, my father had always taught me to treat him with deference. While we were so isolated and alone, I felt less alone than I ever had in my entire life to that point.

Chapter 2

There was a loud knock on the door the next morning.

Alexei grumpily half asleep, "Go see what they want Serg."

I sleepily made my way to the door. The guard looked at me with surprise, as I stood in the Tsar's nightgown. Then he said, "Please inform the Tsar that Mr. Kerensky will be here at 9:00 AM and expects him to be dressed." I went back to inform Alexei.

Alexei, "I think I've had quite enough of Mr. Kerensky." But then he got out of bed and proceeded to get dressed, and I did as well.

Mr. Kerensky popped in without knocking. "Alexei my boy, how are you doing this morning?"

Alexei looked back with a bit of annoyance. "It was going well until now."

Mr. Kerensky, "Come on my boy, the people need to see their Tsar," as we walked out of the room. "Alexei, we are going to walk out to the front gate of the palace and take some photos. You just need to look important and wave at the crowds. There will be protestors outside the gates, ignore them." As we approached the gate, Mr. Kerensky looked towards me, "Wait here this is for me and Alexei alone," then they walked further up and waved as pictures were taken. The reporters had been allowed inside the gate.

A reporter turned to Kerensky, "You really expect us to believe the boy is in charge?"

Mr. Kerensky quipped back, "As much as the English King is."

The reporter then turned to Alexei, "Are you really in charge, or are you Mr. Kerensky's puppet?"

Alexei, "I am the Tsar," he said confidently.

The reporter smiled, "You will make a fine politician someday."

A shout from the crowd barely heard came out, "Death to Alexei, death to the German boy."

Agitators had highly played up the Tsarina's German heritage.

Kerensky, "That is quite enough," as he led Alexei back inside. "Alexei, good job, you may someday make a fine leader yet." Alexei looked on with a bit of confidence and bemusement.

Alexei, "Papa would have never tolerated such disrespect."

Mr. Kerensky, "It is a new day, just ask King George of England how he feels about the press. I have a bit of a surprise for you, we are going to meet your new tutor now. He is a personal friend of mine. I hope you like him."

Alexei, "Mr. Gilliard is my tutor, he has been with me for many years, he is dear to me."

Mr. Kerensky, "We need someone who is going to teach you what you need to know to be a good constitutional monarch, not the old autocratic line."

Alexei, "Papa says a good leader is an autocrat."

Mr. Kerensky, "That is the problem."

We walked into a rather ornate office, where another mid-aged man in a brown suit was smiling.

The man, "Welcome Alexei, good to meet you, my name is Boris Tolstoy, but you can call me Boris," then turning to Mr. Kerensky shaking his hand, "I know you are busy, feel free to go now, I am sure Alexei, and I, will get along just fine."

Mr. Kerensky, "Be good Alexei and do not give him too much trouble, he is here to help," as Alexei rolled his eyes.

Boris turned to me, "What is your name young man?"

I replied, "Sergei."

Boris, "I am here for Alexei, but feel free to pay attention. You might learn something."

Alexei, "Mr. Tolstoy, why do you and Mr. Kerensky treat me with such disrespect, calling me Alexei, when we are not familiar with each other? I was not treated this way as the Tsesarevich, but you and Mr. Kerensky say I am now the

Tsar."

Boris, "Alexei, we mean no disrespect to you, we are trying to instill in you a sense that times are changing, you are better than no other man. We are equal. You may be special, but not superior."

Alexei, "My family has ruled this country for over 300 years, God ordained us to rule."

Boris, "Monarchies ruled other countries as well, but some of them are no more, others have accepted constitutional changes."

Alexei, "Why do you and Mr. Kerensky even want me to be Tsar, when you have such disrespect for my family? You abducted me at gun point, you say I am Tsar, but I am your prisoner."

Boris, "Most prisoners are not kept in a palace. There are those in this country that are Monarchists and that is why we want you to remain Tsar. Kerensky is trying to keep this all from blowing up after your father's mistakes. Kerensky is the only one who has a good dialogue with everybody, the Monarchists, the Democrats, the Communists. He is walking a very fine line, between those who think you are God's hand, and those who want you dead. The people are suffering. Your father mismanaged the Great World War and allowed a crazed monk to influence powers of state. We are trying to alleviate their suffering, while keeping our commitments to our allies in the War. You are a 12-year-old child, a very intelligent mature one, but you are not ready to rule. It is our duty to look after you."

Alexei, "You thought because of my age, I would be the perfect puppet. I visited the front with my father, he was a great leader. Father Grigori was not mad, he was of great assistance to me and my family. He was murdered because people were jealous, he was our dear friend."

I could feel Alexei's agitation, I knew how he worshipped his dad. I remembered Grigori Rasputin whom they called the Mad Monk. I always felt intimidated in his presence, but Alexei loved him. And few knew that Rasputin was the only person who could ease Alexei's hemophilia. To this day I do not know how he did it. Maybe it was God, maybe it was chance, maybe it was his calming influence on Alexei.

Boris, "My Tsar," Boris said in a calming voice, almost as if he felt he had gone too far. "I think that is enough for today. I know these ideas are new to you and leaves you much to ponder. That is part of the learning process. You may be the smartest, most mature pupil of your age I have ever had. You do not have to agree with me or Mr. Kerensky on everything, someday you will become your own man, it is my duty to help you become that man, to think for yourself, not just accept what you have been told to think."

Alexei had that perplexed look on his face, obviously not knowing what to think of this man who he felt was both insulting him and complimenting him at the same time.

Alexei then blurted out, "Can I call Mama, I told her I would, I want her to know I am safe."

Boris, "Mr. Kerensky is in communication with your parents, they know you are safe, but I will see what we can do about that phone call for you." Then Boris walking out and told the guard, "Make sure he is escorted safely back to his room."

After we got back to the room, Alexei sat on the sofa for the longest time petting Joy, who lay next to him. Joy would've never been allowed on the sofa at the Alexander Palace. I sat in the plush chair next to him. Alexei always took the lead. Alexei always determined what we would do and when we would do it. Without direction from him, I felt lost, but I didn't know how to comfort him, so there I just sat.

Then Alexei looked directly at me with his serious look and piercing eyes. "Serg, I want you to speak to me honestly as a friend. Why do people want to kill me? What have I ever done to them?"

I was taken aback, Alexei had always told, he had never asked my opinion about anything before, and as a 12-year-old boy, I didn't really know what to say to him. I then replied. "I really don't know, but I know I don't want anyone to kill you."

Alexei scoffed, "What kind of answer is that?"

I thought really hard, "Maybe they are suffering, and don't know you, maybe they just hate what you represent to them."

Alexei then said, "I wish there was something I could do to help them, but I'm just a 12-year-old boy, locked in a gilded room, being used as a puppet by those who want to tear down my family. There is nothing I can do. Maybe if I play along, I can help the people and my family."

Alexei then sat at the chess board, "Enough moping around, let's play."

Several months passed. Alexei continued his conversations with Boris, sometimes engaging, sometimes irritated, sometimes contemplative. Alexei and I would play chess, or cards. Alexei particularly liked Nain Jaune, a French card game played on a board. Sometimes we would play dominoes. I'm not sure why Alexei enjoyed playing chess with me when I never won. Alexei kept up with his daily diary entries. We were eventually allowed a daily walk in the courtyard, under guard, with Joy of course. This was the highlight of Alexei's day. Kerensky kept tight control of those with access to Alexei, only allowing myself, Boris, and the guards to engage him. The guards grew fond of Alexei as everyone ultimately does. Alexei would occasionally try to invite them to eat with us, or play with us, but they would politely turn Alexei down, saying they wouldn't be permitted to. Kerensky occasionally walked outside with him ceremonially, or put him in front of reporters, under tight control. Kerensky admired how well Alexei played along with the press, never hinting at the disagreements he knew Alexei had. Kerensky and Boris kept "working on" that phone call to Alexei's family that never came, but they seemed to be safe from the little information Alexei gleaned from the newspapers he was given access to. Alexei was Tsar, ruler of all Russia, and at the same time the prisoner of the Provisional Government. But most of the time it was just Alexei, me, and his faithful dog Joy, and in many ways, I enjoyed that, but I knew Alexei was restless, and missed his old life very much. Even as his playmate at the Alexander Palace, Alexei felt like my best friend, but now, even though he was the Tsar, he felt more like a brother to me than my actual brothers. I felt this unexplainable draw to him, like I had never felt before. Alexei could be cranky, and bossy, and even as he called me his friend, he expected me to perform the duties of a servant. But always, his warmth and kindness shined through.

Chapter 3

Then it inevitably happened one night, Alexei shook me awake. His pillow and nightgown were covered in blood, as I looked on in horror. You could see where Alexei had cut off portions of his handkerchief and stuffed it in his nose. He looked pale.

Alexei, "Sergei, I'm bleeding, get the guard." I rushed out to the door to get the guard as Alexei leaned back on the sofa with his head tilted backwards. The guard came in looking somewhat perplexed.

Alexei, "I need a doctor."

The guard, "My Tsar, it looks like you just have a nosebleed."

Alexei, "I need a doctor."

The guard, "I will have my commander contact Mr. Kerensky."

Alexei sarcastically, "Is Kerensky a doctor?"

The guard, "I do not know, but I have strict orders everything goes through him."

I sat next to Alexei on the couch, holding his hand in silence as he petted Joy, who sat on the other end. I knew of his bleeds, but I had never been with him during one. He had always been whisked to his room, visitors, or at least me, not allowed in. That Alexei was a hemophiliac had been a closely guarded secret. We waited for what felt like hours, until around 4:00 in the morning, when a groggy Kerensky finally came through the door. He looked perplexed at Alexei.

Kerensky, "Son you appear to have a nosebleed, that is a lot of blood, but it will stop."

Alexei looked entranced in thought for a moment, not sure what to say. "My Kerensky, no it will not, I am a hemophiliac, my blood does not clot right, I could die. Father Grigori could always stop my bleeding, I miss him so dearly, but now he is gone. I need a doctor."

Kerensky looked as if he had finally realized the hold that Rasputin had over the Romanov family, why Nikolai II had protested so fiercely against Alexei being put on the throne. Some of Nikolai's decisions made some sense in the new light. Everything the family had done to cover up their only boy and the heir to the throne was a sickly child. Kerensky came over to Alexei. "Hold your nose my boy. I will get you the royal doctor. Your secret is now my secret."

Alexei, "Thank you."

Within the hour Kerensky came in with Vladimir Derevenko, Alexei's old doctor, a distinguished looking man with a dark full beard and mustache. Dr. Derevenko's son, Kolya, a chubby boy, was Alexei's best friend, to my jealousy. Alexei seemed to perk up at seeing anybody but me, Kerensky, Boris, and the guards, even as I could tell he was suffering.

Alexei, "Thank you Mr. Kerensky."

Dr. Derevenko, "It is so great to see you again, though I wish it was under better circumstances."

Mr. Kerensky looked perplexed as if the situation was falling out of his control. "Doctor, I do not have time to stay here with you, do what you must, but no politics. And you are not to move him without permission. We must ensure his safety."

Dr. Derevenko nodded grudgingly.

Alexei, "Doctor, how is my family?"

Dr. Derevenko, "They are safe at the Alexander Palace, under tight guard, and miss you so much. Your father is so angered they took you, but there is nothing he can do."

Alexei, "Please tell them I'm fine and in good spirits, and that I love them. How is Kolya?"

Dr. Derevenko, "I will make sure to tell your family. Kolya is good but misses you. Now we need to get you to bed." As he lay Alexei down administering medications and stuffing something that looked like cotton balls up Alexei's nose, he noticed the other wrinkled pillow and turned to me, "You aren't to sleep with the Tsar until he has recovered."

Alexei, "What is going on out there? They keep me on a pretty tight leash. They give me newspapers, but that is all I get, besides an occasional glance through the gates, and what Mr. Kerensky and my new tutor tell me."

Dr. Derevenko, "It is a changing world out there and not for the better, with these radicals running the government. Real Russian patriots want a return to Tsarist rule."

Alexei mockingly, "But I'm Tsar."

Dr. Derevenko tenderly, "You know what I mean my Tsar."

Dr. Derevenko got up, "I shall return, but in the meantime, you get some rest." And then he turned to me, "And you let him get some rest."

Alexei, "Can you pass letters between my family and me? I would love to write to them."

Dr. Derevenko, "It is too risky, they might not let me see you anymore, and the guards keep close track of what goes in and out of the Alexander Palace."

Alexei, "How about Kolya?"

Dr. Derevenko, "Possibly, Kolya would love that, we will need to be careful, but I will see what I can do."

I turned to Dr. Derevenko, "Do you know how my family is?" Dr. Derevenko turned to me. "You are the cook's son?" Me, "Yes," then Dr. Derevenko replied, "Your father is fine and is still with the royal family. To my knowledge the rest of your family is as well." I felt a bit of relief as Dr.

Derevenko walked out.

Alexei, "Get back in bed with me."

Me, "But the doctor told me not to."

Alexei, "It is an order, I'm your Tsar."

I then got back into bed, but with more caution not to bump into Alexei.

Alexei, "But if you hear the door get out, we don't want to get in trouble."

Alexei then leaned back and went to sleep. Days went by as I kept vigil to Alexei. He was weak and pale, and Dr. Derevenko kept on coming. Alexei seemed to greatly enjoy his time with the doctor, saying it was the one upside to bleeding again. And Dr. Derevenko would pass letters between Alexei and Kolya. They largely wrote about mundane things, and how much they missed each other, and hoped to see each other again. He spoke to me very little but expected me to lie in bed with him if no one else was there. I always enjoyed my closeness to Alexei, but felt bad he was ill, and wanted to see him back in his old spirits. Dr. Derevenko largely ignored me, unless to instruct me, but he sure doted on Alexei.

Then one day Kerensky came back, as Alexei was on the mend, and sat on his bedside.

Kerensky, "Alexei, I'm glad you are getting better my Tsar."

I was a little surprised, Kerensky never addressed Alexei as Tsar, except ceremonially.

Alexei, "I'm too. Can Dr. Derevenko continue to come see me once I am well? I'm afraid I might relapse without him."

Kerensky gave his usual response when something was likely not going to happen. "I will see what we can do, but Alexei, I'm going to do you one better. I'm evacuating your family to your Summer Palace in the Crimea. It is safer there, a Monarchist part of the country, and it will help bring greater stability. But before they are moved, I'm going to take you to see them. I'm also going to move you back to the Alexander Palace. You will have the run of the place like the old days."

Alexei had a smile on his face for the first time in days, then he turned serious. "But I cannot be with my family?"

Kerensky, "Sorry, I need you here with me, the peasants need a symbol of the past, yet uncorrupted by it, to keep them out of the hands of the Bolsheviks. Together son, we will save this country."

Alexei, "Can I keep the staff?"

Kerensky, "You wouldn't want to deprive your family of their service? They will be moved with your family to the Crimea. But you have Sergei, and the guards will keep you safe. And we will ensure you are fed."

I was shocked Kerensky remembered my name.

Alexei sighed, "I guess."

Alexei, "How is the political situation?"

Kerensky, "It is a struggle, the Monarchists want my head, the Bolsheviks seem to growingly think I'm a Monarchist, I must be doing something right. Maybe when you get older you will be able to play a stronger role. I'm sure we have our disagreements, but in my time with you, I've come to know you have a heart of gold."

Alexei smiled, never quite sure what to make of Kerensky, as he shifted from bossing him around to flattery.

Chapter 4

Days later Kerensky came for us in his car. The streets were notably quieter than when we came. Over the last several months we had noticed that the shouting had died down. As we got in Kerensky told me to sit up front, that he would sit in the back with Alexei. And we drove back to the Alexander Palace, a big yellow building with white columns, surrounded by very large park-like grounds.

Kerensky turned to Alexei, "Your family is about to be moved to Crimea, as I promised you will get to see them before they leave. But you should keep the conversation positive. You wouldn't want them to worry, would you?"

Alexei responded in one word, "No."

As we rode up to the Alexander Palace, I started to feel a tinge of excitement. The place where I had spent much of my youth with Alexei. The Alexander Palace was different than the Winter Palace. The Alexander Palace, though grand, was also a home. The Winter Palace was very cold and formal. I wondered if I would get to see my dad again. I looked back at Alexei who was very clearly calm in his thoughts. Kerensky was fidgeting and seemed clearly nervous. We rolled up to the big circle drive in front and headed up the steps. The guards as always were fully in tow. We went past the grand halls, and through the library, to the formal family sitting room. The very sunny room had marble-looking walls, a molded ceiling, fancy old-looking furniture, and big old paintings on the walls.

There, sat Tsar Nikolai, Tsarina Alexandra and Alexei's four older sisters. The oldest Olga, then Tatiana, Maria, and Anastasia. Alexei was particularly close to Olga, who was nine years older than Alexei and was like a surrogate mother figure to him. Tatiana was aloof unless you got to know her, Maria was a sweetheart. Anastasia, at three years older, was most often Alexei's playmate of the sisters, and had a mean mischievous streak. We hadn't seen them in months, but they looked different. Nikolai, fully bearded and in a much plainer military uniform than he normally wore looked tired, though he still had a sense of regalness to him. Tsarina Alexandra, quite the beauty in her youth, and whom Alexei clearly had taken his handsome looks from, looked quite sad and ill. Alexei's beautiful brunette sisters seemed stilted. They were normally so lively.

Kerensky, "I am going to give you a few minutes alone, but the guard will remain at the door for everyone's safety," as he headed out. Alexei sat down.

Alexei, "Papa may my friend Sergei sit?"

I wasn't normally permitted to sit in the formal presence of the full royal family, but Alexei still showed deference to his father. In front of Kerensky, Alexei just told me what to do without asking permission. The Tsar glanced at me for a minute slightly surprised and then said, "If you wish my son." I then sat down.

Tsar Nikolai, "I am sorry my dear son that I wasn't able to protect you. But these people now are in charge, and we better do what they say."

Alexei, "Papa, don't worry it hasn't been that bad. I'm sorry they are making you leave. I didn't ask for this. I so want us to all be together."

Tsar Nikolai, "I know, you are not responsible for anything that has happened. Never blame yourself. I tried my best, I did my duty, but you are innocent."

Tsarina Alexandra, "I miss you so much, I hope they are taking good care of you."

Alexei, "I miss you too, I wish I could be with you, they are taking good care of me."

Alexei's sisters started chiming in how much they missed him as well, and in turn Alexei told each one how he missed each one of them. Alexei had been the baby of the family, the Tsar to be, his family's pride and joy, I'm sure they all felt a massive hole in their hearts without him.

Anastasia, "Can I stay with Alexei? I'm sure he is so lonely."

Tsar Nikolai, "I don't think they are going to permit that darling."

Alexei, "I sure wish you could, they call me Tsar, but clearly nothing is up to me."

Tsar Nikolai, "The only nice thing about all of this is I've had some time to work in the garden, read, and not worry about affairs of state."

Alexei, "They haven't kept me very busy either."

After about 30 minutes had passed, Kerensky came barreling back in the room. "We do not want to keep the train waiting. It is time to go."

Alexei, "Five more minutes." With that he stood up and gave every member of his family about a minute hug, and they kissed on the cheeks as he bade them farewell. Their personal things were already packed and waiting outside.

Kerensky turned to Alexei. "My Tsar you stay here. I have some business with you, I will be back in a minute," then he walked out with the rest of the royal family.

As Alexei saw the guard walking behind them, he turned to me, "Follow them, but be discreet." I quickly followed my Tsar's orders. As they walked out the door Kerensky stood back for a minute with Tsar Nikolai, as his wife and daughters were being loaded in the cars.

Kerensky, "I hope you are not going to cause any mischief down in Crimea. We have the Tsar, and any trouble you cause, you cause for him, and his government, and make my job of keeping him safe harder."

Tsar Nikolai turning to Kerensky, "The burdens of state are on your shoulders now. I would never do anything to endanger my beloved son."

Kerensky then turned offering his hand to Tsar Nikolai, and Tsar Nikolai reluctantly accepted as he then headed off. I scurried back to Alexei.

Alexei, "Did you hear anything?"

Not knowing if I should tell him. "Sorry, I did not."

Kerensky then came barreling back into the room and sat down. "Leonid, Sergei's dad is going to stay with you as cook and I'm sure you know Anna, one of the palace maids, will keep the place clean. They will stay here with you, and you can use them how you wish. We will send in gardeners from time to time to keep up the grounds. I've got Dr. Derevenko to remain in the city if you become ill, but otherwise I've need of him elsewhere. Boris will come in on weekdays for your tutoring, we don't want you to fall behind. Food will be brought in for Leonid to cook, it might not be what you are used to, but we are all on a budget these days."

Alexei, "I ate black bread with the soldiers when Papa took me with him to the front lines. You should try it sometime. I prefer simple food."

Kerensky moving on, "The guards will stay on the perimeter of the grounds for your security but otherwise you will have your privacy. We must ensure you aren't abducted by the Monarchists or assassinated by the Bolsheviks."

Alexei somewhat mockingly, "You mean like how you abducted me?"

Kerensky moving on, "I will come once a week at least to have lunch with you, as I'm your Minister, and it is my job to keep you abreast of affairs of state. Any questions?"

Alexei, "Can I have a priest? I haven't gotten to do Liturgy for months. It always brought me great comfort."

Alexei always wore a gold cross around his neck, under his clothes, and took his faith very seriously.

Kerensky, "We will work on finding an appropriate priest, while ensuring your security."

Alexei, "And my 13th birthday is coming up, I want to have a party like the old days, invite some of my old playmates, and cousins."

Kerensky, "You can have a party, we will work on an appropriate guest list while ensuring your security."

Alexei, "Thank you Mr. Kerensky."

Kerensky as he was leaving, "You've a lot more space here Alexei, I hope you enjoy."

The moment Kerensky left, Alexei looked at me with a smile, "Let's go to the phone. I've so many people I would like to talk to." We scurried a room or two down into one of the Tsarina's private sitting rooms where Alexei knew the phone was. He pulled off the receiver to ask the operator to dial someone, but silence. It was dead. Alexei then turned to me slightly disappointed, "They probably cut the line." I had no idea how phones worked or what he was talking about. Then he smiled again, "Let's go see your Papa." We then scurried out of the palace to the kitchen building near the street. I was so glad my dad was going to be allowed to stay. As we came in Alexei jumped in front of me and gave my dad a big bear hug. "Thank you for staying with me, you are one of the few people I've gotten to see in months."

Leonid, "I am glad to be of service to you, my Tsar."

Alexei, "I am going to give you some time to see your son, but when you are done, please bring Sergei's things to my bedroom."

Leonid, questioningly, "Your bedroom my Tsar?"

Alexei, "Yes, Sergei is now my personal attendant and most trusted adviser, I need him near me in case I should need anything."

Leonid, "As you wish my Tsar."

Alexei, "Sergei, when you're finished, we'll meet in my bedroom, I'm going to go find Anna," he said with burst of joy I don't think he had shown since he became Tsar.

I hugged my dad, "It is so good to see you Pa." He hugged me back, then looked toward me sternly.

Leonid, "We must ensure we cause no problems, or I won't get to stay here with you. Mr. Kerensky's secretary vetted all the staff, then personally talked to Anna and me. He made clear if we do anything to stir up Tsar Alexei, it'll be considered sedition, and that we put Tsar Alexei at risk. Be careful what you say to Tsar Alexei."

I felt like I was being asked not to be totally loyal to my friend, but quietly nodded okay.

Leonid, "You go to Tsar Alexei now, he needs you, make sure you follow his instructions and don't give him any trouble. I'll bring your things shortly."

I went to Alexei's rooms. The middle of the Alexander Palace was two story staterooms, such as the Semicircular Grand Hall, the Palace Chapel, and Mountain Hall. There were two wings. The west wing had historic rooms of former Tsars and guest rooms. The east wing was where the family lived, near the side road entrance to the grounds. On the bottom floor the east wing went through the library, the formal sitting room, and then around the corner into the Tsar and Tsarina's personal rooms. On the top floor were Alexei's rooms. First you came to his personal sitting room, then classroom, bathroom, and bedroom, with a door that opened to his playroom in the corner. Then around the corner were his sisters' rooms.

I went to his bedroom as instructed. It was a simple

comfy room by royal standards, yet spacious, with large windows that let in the light, and a religious ikon stand with the images of saints and other religious memorabilia.

Alexei was lying contently on the bed, his dog Joy who had already been brought up was lying on the bed with him. Alexei grinningly, "What should we do?"

Me, "I want to do whatever you want to do."

Alexei, "Let's go find my cats." Alexei was particularly fond of Kotik, a large fluffy tan cat with a black face and paws, who had been given to him while he was visiting the front with his father.

The family dining room was in the library. Later that night we sat down to dinner, and dad was getting ready to serve us. Alexei turned to him. "Set a place for you and Anna, this table is too big for just the two of us."

Leonid, "Are you sure my Tsar?"

Alexei, "Yes, those are my orders."

With that my dad went and got Anna and set their places, as Alexei and I waited at the table.

Alexei, "Let's say grace.

The poor shall eat and be satisfied, and those who seek the Lord shall praise Him; their hearts shall live forever!

Glory to the Father, and to the Son, and to the Holy Spirit, now and ever and unto ages of ages. Amen.

Lord, have mercy!

Lord, have mercy!

Lord, have mercy!

O Christ God, bless the food and drink of Thy servants, for Thou art holy, always, now and ever and unto ages of ages. Amen."

Alexei then went on to tell my dad, and Anna, about everything that had happened to us. I could tell my dad and Anna felt incredibly nervous and out of place to be invited to dine with the Tsar, but Alexei's warmth gradually put them at ease. I knew Alexei missed his family, but I was glad to see him so happy.

We went back to Alexei's rooms where he had spent much of his life. He left his parents' and sisters' rooms largely untouched, almost like a shrine. Except for Tsar Nikolai's bathroom, which had a giant heated swimming bathtub Alexei adored. We headed into Alexei's bedroom, and he played his Balalaika (a Russian folk guitar) before bed. I had always loved listening to Alexei play. Then we went to sleep in his bed, he looked so content.

Chapter 5

As Kerensky promised, Alexei was allowed to have a birthday party. That morning, he came in with eight boys near our age. In introductions, Kerensky explained two of them were his own sons, Oleg and Gleb, and the others were the sons of Duma members. If all went well, we would be allowed to spend other days together. The boys were all in suits and ties, and Alexei in his typical plain military uniform. I had my regular shirt and pants. The boys all called him Alexei and shook his hand, rather unceremonious for a Tsar. Alexei had his typical perplexed look on his face, but then warmly greeted each one of them. Alexei introduced everyone to Anna, my dad, and Joy. For lunch we had tomato cream soup, beef stroganoff, and chocolate cake. We were also served champagne.

Alexei gave everyone the grand tour, showing them the Grand Hall, a huge semi-circular room, where he liked to watch silent films, and Mountain Hall an elegant marble room, which had a wooden slide Alexei loved to slide down. We all went down it multiple times. I think the other boys were surprised to see it in such a grand room. We went up to Alexei's playroom where he showed us all his toys, a train set, boats, airplanes, an Indian teepee and canoes, his toy soldiers and much more.

Alexei grinning, "Clearly there are advantages to being the Tsesarevich."

We went out onto the grounds, Alexei introduced the boys to his cats, and his performing donkey, Vanka. He then showed them his miniature fully gas-powered car that his parents had given him, Alexei's favorite toy.

Alexei, "I would take you fellows for a drive, but I could only fit one passenger at a time. We might as well do something we can do together."

Alexei showed them the Children's Island in the pond, with the full playhouse with leather upholstered furniture, then we walked out to the White Tower, this old castle-looking tower on the grounds. Alexei loved the view from the top, from which you could see the entire grounds, and the surrounding community. It was there on the top of the tower that Alexei decided we were going to all play cards. We sat around playing for several hours. Alexei was the leader of the pack, and by the end of the day, it seemed like we had all been good friends for years. We got to just be boys. Kerensky's elder son Oleg told Alexei that he would like to be Alexei's prime minister someday, and that his dad said Alexei had the makings of a great Tsar. Alexei just smiled. In the end they had all fallen in love with Alexei, like everyone always did. Alexei warmly hugged each one good-bye.

After they left Alexei turned to me. "I wish I could

see my old friends, but they were fun."

I just nodded.

We pretty soon got set into the routine. Boris would tutor Alexei weekday mornings, but otherwise we had the time for ourselves. Alexei treated my dad, Anna, and I like close family. Alexei particularly liked Blini (Russian Pancakes), which he would request my dad make often. Alexei was also fond of Borscht (Russian beet soup). Dr. Derevenko was allowed to visit for Alexei's occasional bleeds. The consolation to Alexei was he got to pass letters between Dr. Derevenko's son, Kolya.

Kerensky's carefully picked friends for Alexei would be brought by regularly. Alexei grew quite close to Oleg, and occasionally debated politics with him. Alexei argued the need for a strong benevolent monarch, and Oleg argued the need for a constitutional monarchy with more democratic rule. But the discussions were always friendly, and Alexei appeared to enjoy the engagement. Often on Saturdays, Alexei's new friends would be brought by, and we would all watch a silent film. Alexei just loved the movies, especially stuff from the United States. Alexei's mom was the granddaughter of Queen Victoria and had spent much time in England. English was her preferred language, and Alexei could speak it perfectly. Alexei would sometimes read the subtitles out loud to us, and sometimes let us guess what was going on. Alexei was also great at French for the French movies. Alexei loved comedies. You could hear his laughter echoing the room, drowning out the rest of ours.

Alexei continued to be cut off from everyone else including his family, and only rarely taken out of the palace for an occasional photo op with Kerensky. Kerensky did provide Alexei some of the correspondence to him from people throughout Russia, and sometimes beyond, especially young people, and Alexei would diligently respond. Alexei took great joy in writing the letters, some of the little contact he had with the outside world, often consoling people for whatever they were suffering. It would break up the monotony. While Alexei was writing his letters, I would often illustrate Alexei's favorite jingles and stories for him. Alexei loved animations and would always compliment my skill.

The grounds of the Alexander Palace were a grand place to grow up, and we spent much time outside. You could tell the season by the trees, as the new leaves came out in spring, it was so green in summer, then the glorious golds of fall, before they bared in winter.

When the weather was warm, Alexei would love to go skinny dipping, and we would often swim out to the playhouse, and hang out there all alone, when Alexei didn't want to be disturbed. I knew when we were there Alexei often wanted silence just to ponder his thoughts. I was careful not to speak unless he spoke to me. But there was something magical just the two of us there in total silence, almost as if the moment was touched by God. Alexei liked to push me in the pond. He thought he was sneaky, but I usually knew he was coming, and I liked to entertain him. Alexei would beg me to push him back, and I was always scared I would hurt him. But after enough begging I would slightly push him, and Alexei would throw himself in the lake.

In the winter, we would build a big bonfire outside and roast potatoes. Alexei loved them stuffed with a lot of butter. He also liked Shashlik (Russian Kebabs). We would build ourselves a big snow mountain that we would go sliding down, and Alexei loved snowball fights. When Alexei's handpicked friends were over, Alexei would insist on snowball fights. I remember the first one as Alexei started throwing snowballs at us, and we started throwing them at each other, but not Alexei.

Then Alexei with a combination of a stern look and a hint of a smile, "Hit me guys, give me your best shot."

We all just looked at him not sure what to do.

Alexei, "Come on girls, I said hit me, I'm your Tsar, it is an order."

Then we all just grabbed our snowballs, and threw them at Alexei, as he stood there still, making no attempt to dodge, but not flinching. As we were done, a huge smile crossed his face.

Alexei, "That is better boys, that is more like it."

After that we never shied away from throwing snowballs at the Tsar of all Russia.

I remember November of 1918, when we won World War I. Alexei was so proud and felt his father had been vindicated. Alexei had spent much of 1916 at the front with his dad. Interacting with those soldiers and seeing the wounded had a deep effect on him. They often took Kolya to keep Alexei company, but I never got to go and was quite jealous. I had missed Alexei for much of that year. Mr. Kerensky took Alexei out for a few more events and ceremonies than usual. At one of the ceremonies Mr. Kerensky was comfortable enough with Alexei by this time to let Alexei answer a few more questions.

Reporter, "How do you feel about winning the war?"

Alexei, "I am so proud of Russia. My father entered the Great War to protect our little brother Serbia from the much larger Austria Hungary. We must always stand up to bullies. I remember spending much time in 1916 at the front with our soldiers, they meant a lot to me, and I wish I could be with them now. I am proud that Russia finished the war."

Reporter, "How do you like the medal the French gave you?"

Alexei, "I earned it in all the battles with my teacher."

The crowd chuckled. "But I do want to thank the French, and all our other brave allies, for all they have done to help us win the war."

Reporter, "The monarchies have fallen in Germany, Austria Hungary, and the Ottoman Empire, and there is now talk of splitting them up into nation states. Do you support this?"

Alexei, "Yes, everybody deserves to live in freedom, and peace, free of oppression."

Reporter, "What about the Russian Empire?"

Alexei, "We won the war together, we can live in peace together."

Mr. Kerensky, "Okay boys, our Tsar is still a young man, enough questions for one day," as he turned around and started walking away.

Alexei, "Wait, it looks like we are done for questions, but I want to thank you all for coming." Alexei then started shaking hands and hugging the reporters.

Mr. Kerensky looking amused turned to me, "Sergei, he will make a fine politician someday."

In that moment it felt as if all Russia's problems would melt away, the mood on the street was jubilant as we drove through it. But Russia was heading into another long Russian winter, with depleted food, fuel, and so much had been destroyed. Soon Russia would slump into a deep

Depression. Alexei tried to keep informed from the newspapers he was allowed. The government was paralyzed, and they couldn't agree on much of anything. The Monarchists wanted Alexei to be a real Tsar, the Liberals wanted to keep him under their control, and the Bolsheviks wanted him dead. I never understood how a living soul could want to kill my kind gentle Alexei, the thought broke my heart. But for the most part, Alexei and I were oblivious to the turmoil gripping the country, as we were kept in our gilded cage at the Alexander Palace, Alexei studied, and we played like normal boys.

Chapter 6

Then came May of 1923, Alexei would be 19 in several months. I could tell Alexei was getting more and more restless. I could feel something was about to happen. But I just enjoyed my time with him, we continued to sleep in the same bed, and I really hoped nothing would change. It was a warm May day, the long Russian winter was clearly over, and everything was in bloom. Alexei and I sat for our usual morning tutoring session, with Boris. Well, it was Alexei's tutoring session, but I found it interesting and enjoyed being near Alexei. I was looking forward to the usual afternoon when Alexei and I would play on the grounds. It was the same room that Alexei had been abducted in so many years ago, in the middle of his lesson with Mr. Gilliard. It is where it all began. Alexei sat at the same ornate table, still in plain army uniform.

As the session drew to a close, Alexei had a very serious look, "Mr. Tolstoy, I'm going to be busy for a while, so your services won't be needed. I will be in contact with you when I'm available again. Thank you so much for your patience all these years and everything you've taught me."

Boris, "May I inquire to what is going to be keeping you so occupied you don't have time for your studies?"

Alexei, "I have some things to do, our country is

suffering. I am the Tsar. I just can't sit and watch."

Boris looking concerned, "Have you discussed this with Mr. Kerensky. He is your minister. As Tsar it is your responsibility to listen to and follow the advice of those with the expertise and experience to run the country."

Alexei, with an air of supreme calm, "I will be discussing it with Mr. Kerensky. Tell him if you must, I'm not going to change my mind."

Boris looking tired, "I know you must think I'm here to indoctrinate you for Mr. Kerensky. But I'm not. Yes, I agree with Mr. Kerensky's vision for Russia and that may be why I was picked. But as I told you the first time we ever met, I hope you learn to think for yourself. We may not agree on everything, but you were always such a smart boy with a good heart, and you have turned into a young man who clearly knows what you want to do. I guess my job is done."

Alexei stood up from his chair, now a slender six feet, two inches, and gave Boris a great bear hug. "Thank you Boris."

Boris, "No, the honor has been mine my Tsar."

I sat there petrified, Alexei often had bounced his thoughts off me, but this was the first time I was hearing this. Alexei had been more quiet for himself lately, and seemed clearly restless, but now I realized action was imminent. I had a strong feeling in my stomach that this wasn't going to turn out well.

Alexei turning to me, "What is wrong Serg? You look like you've seen a ghost."

I asked him, "What are you going to do?"

Alexei with a bit of a mischievous look, "You'll see, trust me, don't worry, I won't let anything happen to you."

With that we walked outside of the Palace, I was slightly curious that we weren't going to have our lunch first, as we always did, but was glad that Alexei and I would have some time to play and forget all this foolishness. Then my heart began to throb again, as we approached the gate.

Alexei to the guard standing at attention, "Take Sergei and me to the Winter Palace please. I need to meet with Mr. Kerensky."

The guard, "We are not allowed to take you anywhere without authorization from Kerensky's office my Tsar."

Alexei, "Do you want me to walk? Mr. Kerensky isn't going to be happy if I'm harmed."

The guard looked scared as if he didn't know what to do. "As you request my Tsar."

We sat down in the car, Alexei and I in the back, and two guards in the front. I was shocked they complied. Was it really this easy? Had we been prisoners all these years for nothing? Was the Kerensky government a paper tiger? We rode through the streets in an unmarked car. The streets were eerily quiet. Alexei had that serene look of calm in his face, a calm I hadn't seen in months, but I was restless.

We walked up the steps of the Winter Palace that we had been imprisoned in from the late winter to the mid-summer of 1917. I never realized Kerensky had his office here, our movements had been so controlled, largely in our little apartment.

Kerensky's secretary tried to announce us, but we just continued into Kerensky's office, unobstructed. I'm not sure how Alexei even knew exactly what door it was.

Kerensky sat back in his chair, more agitated than I had ever seen him, but he didn't seem totally surprised to see us.

Kerensky, "Alexei my boy, what can I do for you today, that couldn't wait until our regular luncheon."

Alexei, "I must do some things, but as my minister, I thought proper to notify you first. First, I'm going to give a speech in front of the Winter Palace, with microphones, and reporters, I also want it on the loudspeakers so a larger crowd can listen. We will announce it to the public so the people can come. Then I want you to arrange a meeting with Vladimir Lenin, and Pyotr Wrangel. We must come together to solve the problems of our country."

Kerensky, "That isn't going to go well my boy. I've never even met with them in the same room. I'm keeping this country together by a thread."

Alexei, "Then I'm going to the Crimea to see my family. After that, on the royal train, I will tour the country meeting my people."

Kerensky, "They will kill you my boy, they will assassinate you."

Alexei, "Trust in God Mr. Kerensky, but I'm not sure if you truly believe in Him. The Duma controls the country and the Army, and you control the Duma. This I know. But even a figurehead Tsar visits his people and tries to bring them together. The people need hope. I will do this with or without your help. Are you going to shoot me? You will no longer have your figurehead. Are the guards going to restrain me? Be careful, you know I might bleed to death, and you will no longer have your figurehead. I'm not going to attempt to depose you, but I will do what I think is right."

Kerensky looking like he was about to vomit. "Well then, I guess I've a lot of preparations to make, now I advise you to go back to the Alexander Palace, I will be by this evening."

Alexei, "Thank you for your attention, but I must make one more request first. I need to use your phone," with that Alexei quickly swiveled towards the phone and grabbed the receiver.

"This is Tsar Alexei, in Mr. Kerensky's office. I need

Tsar Nikolai's place in the Crimea at once please," after a minute, "Hello Papa, I'm going to be down there in a few days. I have so much to tell you about, and look so forward to seeing you, Mama, and my sisters. No don't worry Papa, everything is fine. Give my love to everybody. May God protect you." With that he put down the receiver.

Mr. Kerensky was fidgeting more uncontrollably than I had ever seen him, and the first time I had ever seen him speechless.

We walked from Mr. Kerensky's office. Alexei had such a huge smile, like when he had done something mischievous when he was a child. Alexei was apparently having a grander time than he had in years. I was just dumbfounded, both awestruck and terrified at the same time. I still had this uneasy feeling in my stomach, that it wasn't going to be this easy.

That night we sat in the formal sitting room, waiting for Mr. Kerensky. Alexei had been practicing his speech ever since we got home with an air of confidence, as Joy contently watched him, then we sat silently. Alexei had that look of supreme satisfaction on his face.

Mr. Kerensky walked in, much more somber than his usual self, though he had to some degree regained his composure from the afternoon. He looked tired. Alexei said nothing. Kerensky sat down.

Mr. Kerensky, "I've put great thought into your requests, but there are going to be some conditions. The guards will remain and trail you wherever you go. We cannot risk your security. As your minister it would be an abdication of my duty. The guards have been instructed to follow your command and not attempt to restrict you within reason, under the condition that you aren't to ever be left unguarded. The formal area in front of the Winter Palace will be set up in the morning, two days from now, for your speech. As your chief minister and adviser, I insist that I see it. We'll see how that goes and then I'll see what I can do about arranging your meeting. I'm sure Wrangel will be delighted to see you, but I'm not sure if I can convince Lenin. You may go see your family if you wish, you may travel the country if you wish. This is of course under the condition you aren't destabilizing the government, which will bring about a full-on civil war. Keep in mind the need to be discreet with regards to your family. Your father isn't popular. If people believe you are his puppet, you'll be worthless to this government. And one more thing my boy, if you attempt to collaborate with the Monarchists, and overthrow the Duma, there will be a full-on civil war. Your people will drown in blood. I hope I'm making this clear to you. This isn't a children's game. This government, your government, is the only and I mean only reason that this country hasn't descended into chaos."

Alexei's face had gone from amusement to one of genuine concern. "Thank you, Mr. Kerensky, for everything you've done for me, this government, and the country. I think I understand your requests." Then Alexei went silent.

Mr. Kerensky sat for a few moments in silence. "Thank you," then he and Alexei got up, he shook Alexei's hand, Alexei gave him a bear hug, and then Kerensky left.

Alexei then instructed me to collect the guard.

Alexei, "Mr. Kerensky has made clear you are to follow my commands."

The guard, "Yes my Tsar."

Alexei, "Good, I want to see Father Alexander this evening. I haven't been allowed Confession or Holy Communion for years, it was always such a great comfort to me. I want to see my former tutor Pierre Gilliard, Dr. Derevenko, and Dr. Derevenko's son Kolya in the morning, and I want my phone line fixed. That will do for now, thank you."

The guard, "My Tsar those are not exactly my assignments."

Alexei, "They will have to be for now since you cut my phone line, and I've no one here who would know how to collect them."

The guard, "I will make sure your requests are completed my Tsar."

Alexei, "Thank you for your service, and everything you have done for me."

Alexei was picking up again from his somber conversation with Mr. Kerensky. We had dinner with my dad and Anna, like always. Alexei made clear he was going to be inviting Father Alexander, Mr. Gilliard, Dr. Derevenko and Derevenko's son Kolya to stay with us. And he was so animated in his telling of the day's activities. In fact, I couldn't believe that all of this had happened in a day. My dad and Anna as always were supportive and deferential to Alexei, but you could tell they both looked a bit nervous as Alexei so jovially covered the day's events. Father Alexander, a partially balding gentleman with a long dark beard and black robes was there that night as promised in the Palace Chapel. I was following Alexei as I followed him for so much of my life.

Alexei turned towards me with a slight smirk, "Are you going to follow me to toilet too? This is private, but I'll make sure he stays for you when I'm done."

I blushed violently without saying a word.

Alexei, then in a more sympathetic tone, "I am just teasing you, but this is private my friend." And then he walked into the chapel.

The next morning Pierre Gilliard came in, we met in Alexei's classroom, where he had been held back as Alexei was taken so many years before. You could tell he was delighted to see Alexei again, and Alexei was delighted to see him. Alexei said he was reinstituting him as his tutor, and that Mr. Gilliard would stay in the palace again like the old days. Alexei told him about Boris Tolstoy, whom Mr. Gilliard had never heard of, but Mr. Gilliard conceded he had obviously done a decent job. Alexei said he was thinking about having both Mr. Gilliard and Boris tutor him, but that Boris wouldn't be invited to stay in the Palace. Alexei said he wanted to see a debate between Mr. Gilliard and Boris at some point, he thought that would be grand fun. Alexei then turned more serious and showed Mr. Gilliard his speech. Mr. Gilliard looked at it a bit perplexed.

Mr. Gilliard, "It is a bit liberal coming from you, I remember when you were quite the autocrat. Your father would never give that speech, but you have obviously thought this out, and you are now your own man. Give me a copy and I will write my notes on it for you."

Alexei, "Me a liberal, never," as he laughed, "But we cannot stop all change either, we must do something for the people."

Mr. Gilliard, "You could be a mischievous kid, but you always had a good heart."

Alexei laughed and smiled, "It is so good to have you back, I missed you so."

Mr. Gilliard, "I missed you too, my Tsesarevich, my

Tsar, educating you was the honor of my life."

Then Alexei met with Dr. Derevenko. Dr. Derevenko argued that autocracy shouldn't be abandoned, but conceded Alexei was the Tsar. Alexei argued that this had nothing to do with abandoning autocracy, that this was just about the realities of the day. With Dr. Derevenko of course was Kolya, a plump, talkative young man. Alexei and Kolya jumped into each other's arms in this massive bearhug and greeted each other warmly. It felt as if they had never been apart. I knew before Alexei had been abducted that Kolya was his best friend, not me, but we hadn't seen Kolya in the flesh in years. I felt suddenly threatened that I was no longer going to have Alexei to myself. But I politely greeted Kolya as I always had. Then we had lunch with Mr. Gilliard, Dr. Derevenko, Kolya, and Father Alexander joining us. Alexei's court was growing, though still much lighter than the old days. The Alexander Palace was starting to feel like it used to. Well maybe a little better, the staff used to not eat at the big table.

That afternoon we went out onto the grounds, Alexei, Kolya, Joy and me. I watched Alexei and Kolya play chess, then cards. Then we stripped our clothes and swam out to the playhouse on the island, and just laid around. This was usually Alexei's place of silence, but Alexei and Kolya couldn't stop talking. Back when we were kids Alexei sometimes thought Kolya yammered on a bit much, but now

Alexei couldn't stop catching up with his old friend. We hadn't a care in the world. We had grown into men, but much of our free time remained the pursuits of boys.

Alexei asked Kolya and I, "Do you think we can do it? Do you think we can save Russia?"

I was perplexed, I had no idea how to save Russia, let alone if it could be done, or that Russia even needed saving, or what Russia was beyond my life in St. Petersburg. I hadn't even seen much of St. Petersburg since that day Alexei took me with him into our gilded cage.

Kolya, "Yes, of course, with your leadership we can do anything!"

Alexei, "Sergei?"

Me, "I wouldn't know about those things, but I have faith in you."

Alexei looking as if he wasn't sure about my simple response. "Thanks, my friend, my brother, my advisor."

I felt content.

Chapter 7

We rode up to the Winter Palace and came through the back. As we were walking through the palace to the front, Kerensky came up asking for a copy of the speech. Alexei said he had left it with Kerensky's secretary. Kerensky asked for Alexei's copy to which Alexei replied he had memorized it and didn't have a copy. And we continued to walk through the courtyard, I stood back as Alexei began to wave. The desk sat in back of the gate with the speakers for the crowd, the microphone and the press were all set up. The gates were locked, but the people on the outside were peering in, curious about what the Tsar would say. Never had a Tsar staged an event quite like this. Alexei's father had always been aloof and didn't do these kinds of things.

Mr. Kerensky practically running back up to Alexei, "No speech was left in my office."

Alexei continuing to wave towards the crowds whispered in Kerensky's ear. "We aren't going to do this in front of them are we? And by the way, I don't want you looming over me." He then walked to the desk, pulled the speech out of his pocket, and began to read.

"I am not a Bolshevik, I am not a Liberal, I am not a Monarchist. I am not a politician of any kind. I, unlike the rest of them, did not choose to be here. I am here because my family has ruled over this country for over 300 years, some believe we were ordained to rule by God. I am a Russian and so are all of you. One of my greatest memories as a child was going to the front with my father and eating black bread with the soldiers. I could have had finer fare, but I did not want it, because that was not what a soldier ate. I do not pretend that my privileged life can compare to your suffering, but I have suffered. I was sick many times as a child, and quite often it was thought I would die. I may not have suffered as you have, but I understand suffering. The politicians argue over ideologies that many do not even understand or have never heard of. We are killing each other over ideology. But we all want bread, we all want shelter, we all want safety for our families and to live long healthy lives, and many of us including myself want to believe in God. This country cannot stay the same. My ancestor Peter the Great opened Russia to the West. My great grandfather Alexander II freed the serfs, and once again Russia must change. We must modernize, we must no longer provide for the privilege of the few at the expense of the many. To whom much is given, much is required. If I could achieve this as an autocrat I would, if I could achieve this as a democrat I would. The method is unimportant, what is important is that we do something. That is why I have requested a meeting with Mr. Kerensky, Mr. Lenin, and Mr. Wrangel, because we must come together to solve our problems and create a lasting peace. Then I am going to go on a great tour of this great country and meet you, my people. I know Russia is not Petrograd alone, but a vast sea of peoples. It is in you we will find the solutions to our pain. Thank you, thank you, thank you, it is not your job to serve me, it is my job to serve you."

Alexei then got up waving to the roaring crowd. And then it came.

Alexei, "Guard, open the gates."

The guards looked perplexed, not sure what to do.

Mr. Kerensky went white, "Sergei my boy, we have to stop him, follow me," Then Mr. Kerensky in the most dignified fashion and a serious look, waving to the crowds, approached Alexei with me in tow, and whispered in his ear. "We will be mobbed."

Alexei kind of snickered while still waving and whispered back, "A democrat afraid of his people, trust in God."

I said to Alexei, "If they bump into you, you could bleed."

Alexei whispered back to me, "I have bled before and I will surely bleed again, trust in God."

Alexei then said again more commandingly, "Guards, open the gates," and they did.

Alexei then wandered into the crowd, shaking hands,

giving hugs, listening to people's concerns. Mr. Kerensky just stood there in shock, not fidgeting, not blustering, in total silence, as if he had just seen the Holy Ghost. I didn't know what to make of it, I was afraid they would hurt Alexei, even if unintentionally. We stood there for about an hour, as Alexei's frolic in the crowd didn't seem to end. They treated him between a cross of what we now know as rock stars, and a saint. The Tsar of Russia with his people. Jesus Christ could have come down from heaven and not gotten a warmer reception. He then walked back in still waving to the crowd, and said to both of us, unharmed, "Trust in God," with a bit of a smile on his face. We walked back in the Winter Palace. Kerensky said not a word. He didn't seem happy, he didn't seem angry, he didn't seem sad or mad, just totally expressionless.

On the way out the back door Alexei with a smile jokingly whispered in my ear. "We need to make a law about regular baths and proper dental hygiene." Then we walked into the car.

Before dinner that night Kerensky unexpectedly dropped by, and as always, we sat in the main sitting room. Mr. Kerensky had a pep in his step and was happier than I had ever seen him.

Kerensky, "They loved you my Tsar, they just loved you. The vibe through the city is just electric, the newspapers tomorrow will all be praising you. Even the Bolshevik papers cannot ignore this."

Alexei, with that look on his face as if he had just conquered the world. "You're not angry you didn't get to pre-read my speech?"

Kerensky, "Why no my Tsar, of course not, I even got you your meeting with Wrangel and Lenin. I didn't think Lenin would agree to meet you, but he did after this. You should've done that speech in front of the Duma."

Alexei, "That would've been counter to my point, I did beat you up a little bit."

Kerensky relaxing a bit, "My boy, that is politics, you did what you had to do. I only have one slight concern. You must be more careful with your personal security. You don't know who or what was in that crowd."

Alexei, "Trust in God."

With that they shook hands and Alexei bear hugged him, then Kerensky left.

The expanded dinner table that night with Alexei's growing court was quite lively. Alexei told of his day, but many didn't even need total filling in. It had swept the city. Even staunch autocrats, like Father Alexander, Dr. Derevenko, and Kolya seemed somewhat upbeat. Father Alexander said Alexei was going to save the Monarchy. Alexei had become everything to everyone.

That night as we lay in bed, Alexei appeared intently in thought. I don't know what came over me, if it was impulsive, but I then kissed Alexei on the cheek.

Alexei looked slightly perplexed, "What was that for?"

Russians commonly kiss in greetings, but I guess Alexei felt it was a little out of place.

I blushed, "I do not know, I love you, my friend."

Alexei laughing, "I love you too, my friend." Alexei then waited a few minutes. "You know soon we are going to have to find me a wife. I always liked Princess Ileana. I think that is whom my parents had in mind, but I haven't seen her in years. You'll be married too. And our children will play together. Once I get some more staff here, you'll no longer be my attendant. You'll be my advisor and of course my dear friend." Then commandingly, "Go to sleep now." He turned over on his other side, whether he was still awake or not, I didn't know.

Everything was changing so quickly, I just wanted everything to stay the same. But I never kissed him again. It was never brought up again.

Once again, we rolled up to the Winter Palace, and Mr. Kerensky greeted us. He was more subdued than our last chat with him. Kerensky instructed us to come this way, as we entered the grand dining room with a big table, there sat the angriest, meanest looking man I had ever seen, a balding Vladimir Lenin and Pyotr Wrangel, a distinguished looking older man with a moustache, a man who looked like he would very much fit in with the old elites. Wrangel looked not totally pleased to be there, but very pleased to see Alexei. Mr. Kerensky directed me to sit down in a chair against the wall and sat Alexei at the end of the table. Wrangel and Lenin were opposite from each other, and Kerensky sat on the other side of Lenin.

Vladimir Lenin opened first. "Mr. Kerensky, I have come here today out of respect for you. What exactly do you expect out of this meeting?"

Mr. Kerensky somberly, "This meeting is at the request of Comrade Alexei. I leave the floor to him, I will follow up with you, and Mr. Wrangel, individually at a later date."

Wrangel clearly looked irked at Kerensky's addressing of Alexei. "My Dear Tsar, it is an honor to see you again, I am not sure if you remember me, but I met you as a child. It is so good to see you again. You are clearly connecting with your people, but I must warn you, Russia needs autocracy. Your father knew that. The people are uneducated, and ignorant, they are not qualified to govern."

Alexei, "The people may not be educated, that is why we have the Duma and not direct democracy, but we must look after them, we must care for their needs."

Lenin, looking directly at Alexei, arms folded with his angry little eyes, "Your little stunt was quite amusing. But I came here to tell you this. If you are sincere, if this is not a stunt, leave Russia and take your putrid family with you. The Romanovs have terrorized this country for over 300 years. The people are ignorant, and superstitious, they do need a firm hand from people who truly understand what they need, and that is not you. Leave Russia, while you still can."

Alexei looked taken aback, he had likely never been addressed like this in his life.

Wrangel, "How dare you speak to the Tsar that way Mr. Lenin."

Lenin, "Pyotr, the days of you and your ilk are over, you will soon drown in your own blood, you will be brought to account for hundreds of years of Russian blood, you and your Boy Tsar."

Alexei looked utterly stunned. "I brought you both here today for Russia, because we all care about Russia, we all care about her people, and we must come together as Russians."

Lenin, "I care about Russia and purging her of elitist filth."

Wrangel, "I care about Russia and purging her of communist filth."

Alexei looking helplessly towards Kerensky, "Do you have any ideas on moving forward?"

Kerensky, "This is your meeting comrade."

Alexei, "Why did either of you come here today, if you have no interest in working together?"

Wrangel, "Because I needed to see you. Mr. Kerensky has apparently let you out of your cage, please have your secretary contact me and we can have a more constructive meeting. My apologies my Tsar." He then got up, and walked out, without saying a word to either Mr. Lenin or Mr. Kerensky.

Lenin then got up, "To warn you Alexei, because in that speech I wondered just for a minute, if you would really do the right thing." Then Lenin walked out.

Mr. Kerensky to Lenin, "Comrade, we will talk further later."

After Lenin left the room, Mr. Kerensky turned to Alexei, "I swear that man is going to kill us all someday. Now you know what I have dealt with every day while you play up at your palace, and dream of paradise, my Tsar. I told you I had never met with them in the same room."

Alexei was silent, his heart had sunk. I just wanted to give him a hug at that moment and tell him it was okay.

Alexei, "Why does he hate me so much?"

Kerensky, "He is crazy, that is the kind of craziness

the oligarchs have driven this country to. But he isn't to be trifled with, he has a lot of support."

Alexei, with slightly more optimism in his voice. "But the people love me."

Kerensky, "There is one thing that Wrangel, Lenin, and me can agree on, the people are idiots, they don't know what they want."

With that Alexei got up and shook Kerensky's hand and gave him a sympathetic hug.

"Thank you for trying, I'm sorry if this was a bad idea."

We then walked back to the car, and got in.

I put my arm around Alexei's shoulders, "You're right, the people do love you. They are not the people."

Alexei looked at me with a smile, I think he was a little surprised I was able to put that sentence together, "I know my friend."

Back at the Alexander Palace, Alexei gradually recovered his spirits, after his disastrous meeting, looking forward to seeing his family, and his tour of the country. It was in his speech and wading out into the crowd that Alexei had found himself. I realized that is what he must've been contemplating for several months. Things were becoming livelier at the Alexander Palace, as Alexei now had the freedom to choose who he interacted with. Alexei took up

Wrangel on the audience Wrangel requested. Wrangel made clear that he felt he could get the support of some of the generals in the army, and wanted to make Alexei a real Tsar, but that he had to get him out of St. Petersburg. That once the autocracy had been restored, Alexei could do whatever he wanted, that Alexei, not Kerensky, should be running the country. You could tell Alexei was intrigued by some of Wrangel's arguments, his handsome face with his thoughtful contemplative look. After Wrangel was silent, Alexei sat for a few minutes, before he spoke.

Alexei, "My dear Pyotr, I sincerely appreciate your support for my family for all these years, and your faith in me, but what you are talking about is Civil War. Russia has had enough war, it needs peace. Our choice might not be autocracy, but between the Liberals and the Bolsheviks. Lenin is a scary man. If I must choose between him and Mr. Kerensky, I choose Mr. Kerensky. Mr. Kerensky needs me to legitimize his government. That gives me power to advocate for the changes this country needs."

Wrangel, "You do recognize that Mr. Kerensky and the Provisional Government kidnapped you?"

Alexei, "Yes, my dear Pyotr, we cannot undo the past, I am under no illusions about what Mr. Kerensky has done, but I am willing to work with him for the better of Russia, just as I am willing to work with you, I would even be willing to work with Mr. Lenin if he would work with me."

Wrangel, "My naïve young Tsesarevich, I do wish the best for you. I am at your service."

With that they got up and embraced, and Wrangel was on his way. Alexei even tried to meet with Lenin. Lenin was apparently too busy to meet with Alexei, but he did send his secretary, a man who seemed much more diplomatic than the Lenin we encountered at the Winter Palace, with a letter from Lenin, and a proposal for Alexei. The message was pretty much that if Alexei made some good faith efforts, publicly endorsed the Bolshevik agenda, and stepped down as Tsar, that Lenin would be willing to work with him for the good of Russia. I don't know if Alexei would have stepped down as Tsar, but a strong public endorsement of the Bolsheviks was something he wasn't willing to do.

Before we left Alexei had one last meeting, back in his classroom where he had been tutored for so many years by both Mr. Gilliard and Boris. He just had to put Mr. Gilliard and Boris together before we left, and even brought Dr. Derevenko and Kolya in as well. It was quite a lively conversation. Alexei made clear he wanted the men to speak freely about autocracy vs, liberalism. Dr. Derevenko and Kolya of course staunchly defended the old autocracy, while Boris gave Mr. Kerensky's vision of a liberal government. Dr. Derevenko said that Mr. Kerensky's agenda offended God, while Boris made clear anyone was free to believe whatever they wanted. Mr. Gilliard, fiercely loyal to the Romanov family, and Alexei, clearly had conservative leanings but didn't completely dismiss Boris. It was great fun for Alexei, but in the end, he remained silent on exactly what his own views were. Mr. Gilliard and Boris both shook hands and thanked each other for the role they had played in developing Alexei, both conceded that the other had obviously not done a terrible job, looking at the man Alexei had grown into.

Chapter 8

Then we left the Alexander Palace, as I looked back at the place Alexei, and I had spent so many years. But I also felt a tinge of excitement. While Alexei had been taken on many trips before his kidnapping, I had never left St. Petersburg in my life. In many ways what was to come felt like an exciting new adventure, and with my dear Alexei by my side, I felt like we could conquer the world. The streets were normal, the protesting and riots had stopped. There was a sense of optimism in the air. It was the most exciting day of my life. Alexei was very clearly content, he was going to see his family, then his people. We approached the dark blue painted imperial train, it hadn't been used in years, but it was practically a palace on wheels, with a sitting room, a dining room, and various sleeping suites. Alexei had decided that Mr. Gilliard, Dr. Derevenko, Kolya, Father Alexander and of course Joy would join us. My dad would make sure we were fed, and Anna would take care of the domestic needs. Kolya and I were Alexei's trusted advisors, though to this day, I don't know why he thought the son of his cook was qualified to advise him. As we got on the train a surprise visitor was waiting for us, Oleg, Kerensky's elder son, just a year younger than Alexei, was in a brown suit and the spitting image of a younger version of his father. He had an excited eager look on his face, but Alexei was clearly surprised to see him.

Alexei, as they embraced, "My friend Oleg, what are you doing here?"

Oleg, "I am here if you need any assistance, I hope I can be of help. Your speech was great. I want to serve you."

Alexei, with a not sure look on his face, "Are you here to spy for your father?"

Oleg, "Pa did suggest that you could use some help, but I'm here because I want to be. The guards are perfectly able to keep track of your whereabouts for Pa without me."

Alexei, "Okay, come, you, Kolya, and Sergei will be my advisors, you may be of assistance to me in areas where they cannot."

I was a little let down that Alexei thought Oleg could help him in ways I could not.

Then the train was off, as we barreled non-stop towards the Crimea. I stared in fascination at the countryside, the farms, the forests, the hills, it was all so new to me. Alexei didn't take much interest, he spent much of the time discussing the possible future course Russia might take with Oleg. Oleg was clearly his father's son and defended his vision for Russia. Oleg had a certain idealism of youth, that maybe his father had at one time, but by the time I knew him the responsibilities of the state had clearly worn him down.

We rolled up the hill to Livadia, the traditional
Romanov summer home and palace in Crimea where Alexei's
parents and sisters were being kept. The Crimea was the
Russian concept of paradise by the sea, and a much warmer
climate than much of the country. This was the playground of
the Russian elites. The Crimea was a Monarchist haven. As
we walked up toward the big Italian style palace made of
white limestone and marble, we could see the guard was light
but clearly present. There were palm trees around it, the first
time I had ever seen one out of a pot. In the front, waiting in
anticipation, was Alexei's family. Tsar Nikolai had a resigned
look to him, the look of a once proud man beaten down, but
still trying to maintain a sense of dignity. The Tsarina
Alexandra looked ill. Alexei's sisters were now beautiful lively
young women who looked so full of life compared to the
former Tsar and Tsarina, and they were all clearly just ecstatic
to see Alexei. Alexei warmly hugged and kissed each one of
them. Nikolai firmly shook the hands of Father Alexander,
Dr. Derevenko, Mr. Gilliard and Kolya, clearly delighted to
see them again. He seemed to have some distant recollection
of myself, my father and Anna, he wasn't unfriendly, but also
didn't clearly acknowledge us. Then he looked most
perplexed at Oleg. Tsar Nikolai had never seen Oleg in his
life, wondering whom this young very formally suited young
man was. Then Alexei formally introduced Oleg to his father.

"Papa this is Oleg Kerensky, the son of the Prime Minister and an advisor of mine."

Nikolai slowly assessed this young man with a bit of a look on his face of why on earth would Alexei bring the son of a traitor to his home. Oleg then put his hand out to the former Tsar. Nikolai without saying a word, nodded, and reluctantly shook Oleg's hand. Nikolai then turned his full attention to Alexei, as we walked past the marble columns into the grand home. The wood was lightly colored, and all the big windows bathed the palace in light, there was a certain elegant simplicity to the place.

While we were all permitted to stay in the palace, Alexei made clear he wanted to spend time with his family, and that we would be called upon if needed. My father and Anna slept with the servants, my father helped in the kitchen, and Anna helped with the domestic work. Oleg and I were given a room to share, and for the first time in many years, Alexei slept alone. Dr. Derevenko, Kolya, Mr. Gilliard and Father Alexander were occasionally invited to the family table, and once or twice Oleg and me. Though unsaid, the mood seemed clear that Oleg and I were to be seen but not heard. I wasn't being treated with any particular importance, but unlike my dad and Anna, I wasn't being treated like a servant either. The family was clearly enjoying themselves, but it had a very different feel than the lively conversations that were had at Alexei's table at the Alexander Palace. Alexei's table had such a collection of people, where Alexei the center of attention would entertain his court. The former Tsar, though not disrespectful to Oleg, never said a word to him. I often saw Tsar Nikolai puttering in the garden, and he had taken up carpentry. He had always enjoyed the simpler things in life, and now he had the time to do them. Nikolai had been the son of a Tsar, but I think he might have been just as happy being the son of a peasant.

Often after dinner, Tsar Nikolai and Tsar Alexei would sit out on the porch looking at the sea, drinking port wine and smoking cigarettes. Though there have been vicious rumors that Nikolai was a drunkard, he never had more than a glass. They would sometimes talk, but quite often sit there in silence. Nikolai for the man who had been Tsar seemed resigned to fate, and not particularly concerned about the affairs of state. Nikolai did express deep concern for Alexei's safety, and that he was being used as a puppet by the Duma, but he didn't argue with Alexei. Tsar Nikolai though he seemed to deeply regret he wasn't able to prevent Alexei from being taken, had come to deeply respect the man Alexei had become, even if their views diverged.

I got a lot of time to myself, which I spent on the beach, often with Oleg and Kolya, and we seemed to be here without a purpose. It felt like paradise, though I did miss being Alexei's shadow. I had probably not spent more than an hour or so away from him, unless for one of Kerensky's photo ops, since Alexei was taken. Oleg, Kolya and I often laid on the beach in silence, I had known them for several years, but we didn't have a ton in common, besides Alexei. But that was fine, we were in paradise, I had seen the cold dreary Gulf of Finland, but this was different.

Occasionally Alexei would come down to go skinny dipping in the ocean with us. I remember the first time, Alexei, Kolya and I were stripping our clothes, knowing the drill, and it was pretty clear that Oleg planned to jump in fully clothed. Alexei had that famous grin on his face when you knew he was amused and chuckled.

Alexei, "Oleg take your clothes off, you don't want to get them wet."

Oleg looked at Alexei, unsure, blushing.

Alexei, "Come on swimming is more fun naked, if the Tsar of Russia can strip, you can. We are all guys, there is nothing we haven't seen before."

And with that Oleg relaxing, but not saying a word, stripped his clothes and we all jumped into the sea.

What was supposed to be a few days became close to three weeks, though I knew Alexei was greatly excited about his tour, in many ways he didn't want to leave, just wanting one more day, then another, then another. Finally, it was time to go, Alexei gave his family warm hugs and kisses on the steps of the palace to say goodbye.

Then Tsar Nikolai approached me, "Sergei, thank you for your loyalty to my son for all these years."

I was in shock, and intimidated, at the same time. I just bowed, "Thank you my Tsar." Tsar Nikolai then shook my hand and turned back to Alexei. Alexei hugged each family member a second time, and we were off to the train. Alexei was off to his rendezvous with fate.

Chapter 9

Alexei's first speech was in Yalta near Livadia, and this speech, like his ones to come, were very similar to the one he gave in St. Petersburg at the Winter Palace. It might've been a slightly liberal speech for this Monarchist stronghold, but Alexei was revered, and they greeted him with excitement. Alexei, like in St. Petersburg, and all his speeches to come, waded into the crowd, shaking hands, hugging, listening to people's concerns. Alexei always took a particular interest in children, often squatting down to their level, or if small enough lifting them up into his arms. Many in the audience looked as if they had been touched by God. Kolya, Oleg and I would always watch in awe, as Alexei, our dear friend, who had always so endeared us, put his natural charm to work on the masses, using his God-given talents in his quest to build a better, kinder, gentler, freer, more inclusive Russia for all.

Then the train was off as we weaved through Ukraine. Some of the stops along the way were little villages. At each little station we would get out and Alexei from the platform would give his speech to the crowd. As always, the crowd would roar, and then inevitably Alexei would wade into it. Alexei truly was the people's Tsar. With his simple message, charisma, warmth, youthful good looks, and symbolic importance, he won them over. His plans were not complex, his promises were few, but he cared, and brought a message of real change. Alexei would often jokingly make a quiet remark to Oleg, Kolya, and I on the people's hygiene on the way back to the train. Oleg and Kolya would roar with laughter. Clearly, they believed in the people, but would never truly be of the people. But if Alexei was in any way put off by the smells of the crowd, he didn't show it while with them. He fed off their energy and basked in their adoration. I'm not sure if Jesus descended from heaven, if he would be more adored than Alexei was. If we came to a more important town, Alexei would visit important landmarks or talk to the local administration, under the weak control of the Duma. Evenings were spent with Alexei and Oleg deeply engrossed in conversation.

Alexei had always enjoyed his debates with Oleg, but they were becoming deeper. Oleg seemed to truly believe in Alexei's leadership value, but also was ingrained in the liberal ideology of his father. Kolya would yammer on in support of Alexei, until Alexei gave him that look to knock it off. I would just sit there beside them in silence, along with Joy, whom Alexei was often quietly petting. Like Joy I didn't have much to add to the conversation, but I believed in Alexei. Alexei often considered Gilliard the authority on a more technical point. Dr. Derevenko was there in case Alexei had a health issue, and Father Alexander for Alexei's daily prayers and communion. My father handled the food, and Anna attended to everyone's personal needs. While all the guards couldn't come at once, Alexei insisted that a different guard would have dinner with us each night. It was Alexei's way of showing his appreciation for them, and like everyone who was graced with Alexei's presence, they came to love him like a brother.

While confession was always private, Alexei would always invite Oleg to pray with him. Oleg had some concept of prayer but looked clearly uncomfortable. I never quite understood, the rest of us were good Christians, but Alexei always wanted to pray with Oleg, whom while I never quite knew what his religious faith was, clearly had secular views. It almost became Alexei's personal crusade to turn Oleg into a good practicing Orthodox Christian. While Oleg never directly rejected religion in their conversations, he clearly believed in a secular state. I remember one of their debates.

Alexei, "The Russian people are a devoutly Christian people, we want to believe in God, Russia is lost without faith, we must not abandon Christ."

Oleg, "Not all Russians are Russian Orthodox, what about their rights?"

Alexei, "That is fine, Mr. Gilliard is Protestant, we are all brothers in Christ."

Oleg, "Not all Russians are Christian, what about their rights?"

Alexei, "It is the duty of every Christian to peacefully, with love, share the good news, to bring every heart to Christ."

Oleg just sighed, knowing he was never going to convince Alexei, and Alexei with his smile you could tell felt he had won the debate. And Kolya and I concurred with Alexei, but looking back on it, I have to give Oleg credit, he was brave in being the lone voice of dissent, in his vision for a truly equal Russia. But then Alexei's good heart made it easy to share with him, even if you knew Alexei wasn't going to agree with you. As Alexei and Oleg bonded, I always felt a bit left out.

We rolled into the Kiev station, Alexei did his thing, and then we sat back down in the train's sitting room. A small, dignified, elderly looking woman, dressed in black, with a big fur coat, walked briskly on to the train. I hadn't seen her in years, but I remotely recognized her as the Dowager Empress and Alexei's grandmother.

Alexei jumped up and ran to her, shouting, "Babushka," as they hugged and kissed on their cheeks.

Then they sat down clearly delighted to see each other.

Babushka, "I would've come down to see you at

Livadia, but your mom and I never really got along."

Alexei, "I understand, but least we get to see each other now. I have missed you for all these years. I have really missed so many of my family and friends since I became Tsar. We have been separated for too many years."

Babushka, "I tried several times to see you at the Winter and Alexander Palace, but they wouldn't let me through."

Alexei, "Don't worry about it, they didn't let anybody through. There was nothing I could do."

Babushka, "I know it was that scoundrel Kerensky."

Oleg looked slightly tense, but kept his face, it is unlikely the Dowager Empress realized that the young man sitting several chairs to the side of her was the son of the Prime Minister.

Alexei, "I am under no illusions about the past, but I think we can build a better future."

Babushka, "I know Pyotr Wrangel came to see you, he very much wants to help you. This country is descending into anarchy. The Liberals cannot save us. The Bolsheviks are out of control. We need a strong hand. Your father and grandfather understood that."

Alexei, "I don't control the powers of state, and I do appreciate Pyotr's loyalties, but his plan will create a Civil War. The past is gone, but we can look to the future. We must bring this country together, bring our people together, only then will we save Russia."

Babushka, "My dear sweet Tsesarevich, you were always such a good tender-hearted child. I have missed you so. Come have dinner with me at my house, just the two of us. We won't talk politics. I just want to see you."

Alexei, "I can spare a few hours, a few of the guards will trail me, they aren't going to let me go alone."

Babushka, "Of course, your safety comes first. The streets are crawling with radicals."

And with that Alexei left the train with his grandma and Joy, while the rest of us stayed behind, somewhat lost without our sun, the center of our universe. As always with Alexei, a few hours turned into a bit longer, and dinner turned into breakfast and lunch. Alexei didn't come back until the next afternoon. To this day I don't know what they talked about, or did, but Alexei was in very high spirits on his return, and clearly enjoyed his visit.

In Minsk, after Alexei's speech, and romp in the crowds, as we approached the train, an elderly man with a long white beard, dressed in black, with a black hat, approached Alexei. He was a Jewish Rabbi.

Rabbi, "My Tsar, may I speak with you?"

Alexei, "Come on in with me and sit down with us."

And we walked inside and sat down in the train's

sitting room.

Rabbi, "My Tsar, I want to thank you for all you have done, to abolish the Pale, and to grant equal rights to your Jewish citizens."

The Pale was the areas in Russia where Jews were allowed to live.

Alexei, "I have not been heavily involved in the details of state, who you should really be thanking is Prime Minister Alexander Kerensky, he is not here, but here is my trusted advisor and son of Alexander Kerensky, Oleg."

Oleg got up and shook his hand happily. The rest of us sat with fear and apprehension. We had all heard the many myths of the day about the Jews, and their sinister deeds, and plans. But Alexei and Oleg seemed unconcerned.

Rabbi, "Thank you Mr. Kerensky, and your father, and the Tsar, for everything that has been done."

Alexei, "I would very much like to come to your synagogue if that is okay with you. I would like to come to know the Jewish citizens of the Empire as much as I know our Christian citizens."

The rest of us, except for Oleg, went white.

Rabbi, "We would be honored with your presence my Tsar. We are having service tomorrow evening, and it would be an honor for you to be there."

Alexei, "I will be there, thank you very much for the

invitation. Would you like to have tea with us?"

Rabbi, "I sincerely am grateful for the offer, but I am in observance with very strict Kosher dietary rules, so I am unable to, but I can sit with you while you have tea if you like."

Alexei, "It is okay, I know you are a busy man, I look forward to seeing you tomorrow."

With that Alexei extended his hand and they warmly shook hands. And the Rabbi left. As Alexei sat down petting Joy, Mr. Gilliard sat next to him.

Mr. Gilliard, "My Tsar, you know the Jews cannot be trusted, they killed Christ, and your great grandfather, they are plotting world domination, just read the Protocols of Zion."

Alexei, "Jesus was a Jew, we cannot blame a whole race for the actions of a few. I'm familiar with the Protocols of Zion, it sounds like paranoid rubbish to me. I bet our Jewish citizens are just like our other citizens, they want to live in peace and prosperity, and a better world for their children. The Bible says to love your neighbor as yourself. Our Jewish brothers are our neighbors."

Mr. Gilliard, "I fear for your safety."

Alexei, "Trust in God, I truly appreciate everything you have done for me, and I know you speak out of concern and love for me, but my mind is made up. Now let's move on to something more pleasant."

Alexei had never so strongly challenged Mr. Gilliard before, Alexei always had great reverence and respect for him. We all sat in silence drinking our tea, pondering what Alexei had said. Oleg just beamed with pride, he was so proud of Alexei. Alexei seemed deep in thought for a bit, but quickly decided we were all going to play cards. Alexei could only take being serious for so long, and always knew how to lighten the mood.

The next evening, Oleg, Kolya and I went to synagogue with Alexei. The Rabbi introduced Alexei as an honored guest, and then Alexei stood in silence as service was conducted, intently absorbing it all. Afterwards, Alexei greeted the members of the synagogue, shaking hands, and with hugs as always. Then we were invited to share a Kosher meal with them. Alexei sat next to the Rabbi, asking questions about some of the things he had seen in service, and the Rabbi politely answered. Many of the members seemed deeply moved and touched by Alexei's considerateness and respect. Some had tears in their eyes. The Tsars of Russia had never been a friend to the Jewish people, but then here was Alexei, the Tsar of all Russia, he was clearly different. And Alexei didn't mention his deep Christian faith once the entire evening.

Oleg made sure his dad knew everything that had happened, and Mr. Kerensky made sure the Jewish newspapers knew. A new day in Russia was dawning. Then the train took a sharp east turn heading into old Russia, towards Moscow.

Chapter 10

Then we came up to Moscow, I was amazed by the grand old city, but Alexei had seen it before. Alexei took a motorcade through the streets, waving to the adoring crowds, with the Mayor of Moscow seated beside him. Alexei took confession and Holy Communion at St Basil's Cathedral, the famous story book looking church, with the colorful domes. Then Alexei came out front where everything was set up for his speech, this was the biggest crowd yet. Like always Alexei hit on similar themes. The crowd roared so loud I'm sure it was heard in heaven. And Alexei once again did his thing, giving the people a piece of their Tsar.

Oleg called his father from the train station. As we were headed back on the train. He ran up clearly elated.

Oleg, "Pa is ecstatic, he says it is working, that he might be able to truly get some real reform through the Duma, even the Bolsheviks are becoming cautious about openly criticizing you. We are doing it, we are doing it."

Alexei jumped on Oleg with one of his famous bear hugs. "Thanks for the news, when you are on the phone with your Pa, make sure you give him my good wishes."

Oleg, "Don't worry, I do, but Pa is concerned about your security, there are still radical elements out there, and Pa is concerned they may view your popularity as a threat."

Alexei, "Trust in God my friend."

As we boarded the train, Alexei began to noticeably limp, something he had concealed before with great grace. I became immediately fearful. When Alexei showed signs of pain, it usually meant he was bleeding.

Oleg, "Are you okay?"

Alexei, "I'll be fine."

Alexei then called for Dr. Derevenko. Alexei sat down on the couch, stripping his simple military uniform down to his underwear. The gold cross hung around his neck.

Alexei, "I was bumped in the crowd."

Dr. Derevenko, "You really got to be more careful." As he carefully examined Alexei, right above Alexei's foot, around his ankle, a bruise was clearly forming. "You are bleeding my Tsar, we must go back to Petrograd, you must get some rest."

Alexei, "No, I must continue, treat me the best you can, but we must continue."

Oleg was looking perplexed. "It is just a bruise, it will heal."

Alexei, "I am a hemophiliac, my blood doesn't clot right, but do not worry my friend, this has happened before, I'll be okay."

Oleg, "Does Pa know?"

Alexei, "Yes, he does, I had a nosebleed shortly after

he kidnapped me, and held me in the Winter Palace. He has known ever since.”

Oleg, “Maybe we should go back to Petrograd then,” looking clearly concerned.

Alexei, “No, Trust in God.”

Oleg was the only one on the train who didn't know about Alexei's hemophilia, his father had clearly kept the secret well. Though I worried about Alexei, I stood in silence. I knew once Alexei had made his mind up that there was no changing it. Even though Alexei wouldn't go back to St. Petersburg, Dr. Derevenko was able to convince Alexei to at least rest on the train a few days, while he treated it. He told Alexei that if the bleed got worse, his public engagements would be in a wheelchair. And with that, things slowed down a bit. I was glad we would get a bit of rest.

That night after dinner, Alexei asked me to come to his private room. He told the others he needed to confer privately with his advisor. Once we got in, Alexei set up the chess board and sat at the little table.

Alexei, “Come play with me.”

Me, “I am sure Oleg and Kolya are better chess players than me.”

Alexei with his famous smile, “I do not care.”

And we started to play, and for the first and last time ever, I won, I don't know how I did it, I'm not even sure if

Alexei didn't let me beat him. Then as the game concluded.

Alexei, "Serg, I know you've been feeling left out lately, for that I'm sorry. Oleg is a great friend and a lot of fun, and Kolya is my best childhood friend, but we grew up together. You'll always be my greatest advisor."

Me, "Thank you my friend, my brother, my Tsar."

Alexei, "Come to bed."

It was the first time Alexei had wanted me to sleep with him since we left the Alexander Palace.

Me, "You know I'm not supposed to sleep with you while you are bleeding, I could accidentally bump into you."

Alexei, "Trust in God."

I put out the lamp and laid down on one side of the little bed, Alexei turned to the opposite side of me. It was much smaller than I was used to, but we fit. I'm not sure how Alexei knew I had been feeling left out, but he did.

Alexei, "Now go to sleep."

I knew this was Alexei's way of saying to be still, and not make any noise. It is the last time I would ever sleep with him, but Alexei did make a little more effort to make me feel included with Oleg and Kolya.

Within a day or two Dr. Derevenko still had some concerns, but Alexei was insistent that he felt well enough to continue. We turned east heading toward the Ural Mountains and Siberia, a place not often visited by the Russian Tsars, but

Alexei felt he couldn't be the Tsar of just one Russia.

We rolled into a little town, and Alexei got out and did his thing. At the end a simple man of little stature told Alexei he was the representative of some little hamlet and would be honored if the Tsar would accompany him. That is if Alexei wanted to see the real Russia. Alexei agreed to go, and Oleg, Kolya and I accompanied him. One of the guards drove Alexei, Oleg, and the man in the first car. While another guard drove Kolya and I in the second. The rest of the guards were in a truck in the back.

We rolled into this little hamlet that looked untouched by time. The people seemed very interested in our vehicle, as if they hadn't seen motor cars much. The houses were tiny and unpainted. The furniture was simple and wooden. They had no extras in life, no electricity, no running water, no toilets, no telephones, they didn't even appear to have games to pass the time. The people were dirty and very thin. But to them Alexei was like a God. Once the little man made clear they could share their concerns with Alexei, they told Alexei about how they could barely feed themselves, and could barely get the fuel to warm themselves, through the long Russian winters. Little was left after paying the landlord. Their children were not educated, and they had little access to healthcare. Alexei, Oleg and Kolya were all in shock at the stark contrast to Alexei's extreme privilege, or the upper middle-class lives of Oleg and Kolya. Even I had spent my life in St. Petersburg, my father on the royal staff, and I wasn't prepared for this.

Alexei intently listened to them all, with a look of such deep concern on his face. Gone were the smiles and his usual jovialness. You could tell Alexei felt their pain. Then with a much simpler speech, Alexei spoke to the crowd.

"Until today, I realize now that I did not truly know the real Russia. I have had a very privileged life, but to whom much is given, much is required. I want to thank you all, from the bottom of my heart, for introducing me to the real Russia, to your struggles, to your pains. For Russia will not be judged by the wealth of the few, but the suffering of those who have the least. We need true land reform. We need a system that will provide for the welfare of all. I promise you from the bottom of my heart, I will do everything in my power to help you."

With that they all dropped to their knees, as if they were about ready to pray to Alexei.

Alexei, "Rise please, rise, I do not want to see anybody on their knees. We are all equal in the eyes of God, and we should all be equal before the law. From the Tsar to the meekest peasant, in the new Russia we will all be equal."

They slowly arose with tears in their eyes as Alexei passed among them, hugging them. Alexei impeccably groomed, hugging these unkept farmers. You could tell they were truly touched by this caring, simple Tsar.

We rode back to the train station. Oleg was heading into the train station to call his dad.

Alexei, "Tell your Papa we must do more to implement land reform now. This cannot wait. Also tell him, I want an inventory done of all the royal property. We can sell what my family and I aren't using and use the funds to help the poor."

Alexei, Kolya and I sat down in the sitting room of the train, Alexei was petting Joy. Oleg came back and sat down with us.

Oleg, "Pa says he is working on land reform, but it is tough, Conservatives in the Duma are doing everything they can to block anything meaningful, and Pa is concerned about their influence with some of the generals in the army. Pa says you being willing to sell royal property is a sheer stroke of political genius, and he will start on that project right away, but that ultimately it is a drop in the bucket of funds needed to truly help the poor of this country."

I could tell Alexei looked a little disheartened. Kolya and I both started telling Alexei what an amazing Tsar he was, how much he cared, how much the people loved him, which clearly cheered him up.

Mr. Kerensky made sure the press had every detail of

the day. Alexei was truly becoming hailed as the people's Tsar. And I have to give Alexei, after that day, he never made fun of the crowd's hygiene again.

Chapter 11

The train came rolling into a small station shortly before the Ural Mountains. The crowd was a little smaller, but still ecstatic as Alexei gave his remarks. But now he was putting a little more emphasis on land reform, and that those with much must contribute more to help the poor. It was warm for what we thought of the region, but it was summer. Alexei then waded into the adoring crowd. The sun was bright.

As Alexei got back up on the platform, and we headed back to the train, a man who seemed out of breath, as if he were late for an appointment, said, "My Tsar." Alexei turned to greet the man, his face filled with warmth and friendship. The man pulled out a pistol and Alexei's face went white. One of the guards grabbed the man and soon the rest piled on.

Alexei regained his composure, "Do not hurt him."

The guards looked as perplexed as the crowd, while still restraining the man, but they eased up a little bit. Oleg, Kolya and I still looked like we had seen the Holy Ghost.

Alexei walked up to him with the most serene but subdued composure. "Sir, I know you do not hate me, but you hate what you think I represent. I truly hope that I can prove to you that I am sincere, that I want to reduce your suffering. The only thing I can promise you is I will try my best to help you. I hope someday you will no longer see a need to kill me. Go with God."

The man looked stunned as Alexei treated him with kindness and love.

Alexei turned to the guards, "Take him somewhere he is safe, make sure he is disarmed, then let him go. He has not hurt me. You cannot have a crime if you have no harm."

Everyone was stunned, but the guards complied with Alexei's orders, as we walked back into the train. Oleg, Kolya and I were still stunned, but Alexei was calm.

As we got on the train and sat down Oleg tried to speak. "While you were busy speaking, I spoke with Pa on the train station phone. He is elated by the responses, but as we head into the Urals, he is seriously concerned about your safety. It is a hot bed of Bolshevik activity. And he fears your safety cannot be provided for. After that event, I'm afraid he might be right."

Alexei, "Trust in God."

Oleg, "Pa was afraid you were going to say that. He says at the very least he is upping your guard, and he is putting an advance car on the tracks in case there is a bomb."

Alexei, "So the person operating that car gets blown to bits instead of me?"

Oleg, "Yes that is kind of their job. You are the Tsar.

We cannot lose you."

Alexei, "Your Pa does as he wishes, if he wants an advance car, I doubt there is much I can do to stop him."

Oleg, "Thanks."

Alexei, "Thanks for what, I didn't give my consent, I merely recognize that I'm not in a position to stop your father."

Oleg, "Okay, I think Pa can live with that."

Oleg, "Why did you let that guy go? He is a criminal, he should've been brought to justice under the law, we are Liberals, not Anarchists."

Alexei, "Your Pa kidnapped the Tsesarevich of Russia. If he wasn't successful in his takeover, he would've likely been executed for treason, but I have forgiven him. That guy who tried to kill me, maybe if you lived in his shoes, you would've tried to kill me too. Both of us have come from privileged backgrounds, we've had everything in life. We cannot begin to feel their pain."

Alexei, changing the subject, "It'll be my birthday soon, we won't make it back to Petrograd, but we should have a party."

The rest of us were still all a little stunned to be thinking of a party, but as always, we concurred with Alexei. I thought of the man who had tried to shoot Alexei. I wished I could have bashed his head in with my fists, but I knew we must respect Alexei's wishes. I thought the scum was not worthy to kiss Alexei's feet.

The mood on the train had grown somber, but Alexei was his usual self. Alexei's bleed was still not totally gone, but minor compared to some of his previous bleeds. Dr. Derevenko kept a tight wrapping right above Alexei's ankle, which seemed to have slowed it. The train was heading up into the darkly forested Ural Mountains. Alexei discussed the future with Oleg, Kolya, and Mr. Gilliard, making sure to include me as well, but I was having a hard time thinking about politics. I could only think about Alexei. As the nightly paper was delivered to the train, it was clear that the story of the people's Tsar who had forgiven his assassin had spread through the country like wildfire. Alexei was even more popular than ever. Oleg thought the story could undermine the sense of justice, though his father Mr. Kerensky was clearly responsible for ensuring the press got a hold of it. Oleg suggested that maybe the train should be turned around, and we should head back to St. Petersburg for Alexei's safety, Mr. Gilliard and Kolya concurred, but Alexei was determined to forge ahead. I was silent, I knew by then there was no purpose in arguing with Alexei when his mind was made up.

Oleg looked at the schedule. "Has anybody ever heard of Ekaterinburg? It looks like we'll be there on July 17th."

Alexei, "No but the villages are important too, like the many we've already visited. Russia is not just the cities. We'll work our way through Siberia, it'll be great fun. I can't wait to see the home village of Father Grigori. And on to the Pacific Ocean. I've never been to Siberia before or seen the Pacific. On our way back I want to loop through some of our Central Asian provinces and meet some of our Muslim subjects. They are a part of the Empire too."

Alexei paused.

"You know my Birthday will be August 12th, I'll be 19 years old. I wonder what kind of party we can throw in Siberia."

Mr. Gilliard, "The train is well stocked, I'll work with Leonid to make sure it is a special day for you."

Alexei, "Thanks."

Thinking of Alexei's birthday, we were all feeling a bit up again. Then Dr. Derevenko checked Alexei's bleeding, it had stopped. Father Alexander thought it was a good omen, and said Alexei was blessed by God.

Alexei then drifted on to the future, "It would be great fun to visit the world someday, the Holy Land, New York, I've always been fascinated with America, I always looked forward to the next edition of the "Mysterious Hand of New York" to come out, maybe see the Wild West. Papa always talked about visiting Japan, he even got a tattoo. I doubt Dr. Derevenko is going to let me have one," as he smiled, "but I'm probably going to be too busy with Russia for a while, it feels like I could travel the Russian Empire forever, and only see a small part of this great land."

With that Alexei insisted we were all going to play cards and ordered the champagne to be poured just for fun. Alexei always knew how to have a fun time.

We pulled into Ekaterinburg. It was July 17th, 1923, a date many very well know. We had arrived a little early, and Oleg made his phone call to his father at the station. He came running back, I had never seen him so excited. "Pa is astounded, he says Mr. Lenin is ready for a true reconciliation, that the Bolsheviks are speaking positively about you, even in their papers. They are even calling you Comrade Alexei. Mr. Lenin says he will even meet with the Monarchists if you are present."

Alexei with that look of supreme satisfaction on his face. "We have won, we will bring the country together. I have restored my family's honor. I will go down like my ancestors, Peter the Great and my Great Grandfather Alexander II. I have always so admired my Great Grandfather, you know he freed the serfs."

Mr. Gilliard had a perplexed look on his face. "My Tsar, you are a great leader, I so admire the man you have become, but I'm not so sure it is going to be this easy."

Dr. Derevenko, "My Tsar, Lenin is a snake, he cannot be trusted. Please I beg of you, do not let that man fool you."

Me, "My Tsar, I trust in you, I believe in you, I have faith in you, if you say it is, then it is."

Alexei, smiling, "I think I have to rate Sergei as the winner of this debate," he said with a chuckle. Alexei then squatted down giving Joy an extra-long pet. "My dear advisors, Oleg, Kolya, Sergei, I think it is time." We walked out of the train together, all four of us feeling on the top of the world, but Alexei was truly on top. As we walked out on the platform it was such a beautiful warm day, the sun was shining, it felt like heaven had touched this little spot in the Urals, how could such a beautiful place be filled with people who would want to harm such a great man. Alexei stood on the platform in his simple military uniform, with the red bars on his shoulders. And then his speech began. I don't know if it was because of the extra confidence he got from the news, or because he had done it so many times, or maybe that his bleed had stopped. But in that moment, it was almost as if I was watching God. Oleg, Kolya and I stood behind him full of confidence, glowing ear to ear. This was the best one, in St. Petersburg, I was in terror when he first did it, but now in this moment, I knew to trust in Alexei. God's will would be done. His speech remained simple, not a lot of proposals, not a lot of concrete plans, but it dripped hope, and in that moment, I knew that is what the people truly wanted, hope. The crowd roared, and then Alexei went down as he always had to greet his people. The day felt special, Alexei's warmth oozed, Alexei always tried to be in high spirits, but I could tell today he wasn't pretending. It was if Jesus himself had walked into that crowd.

I noticed he knelt and picked up a little boy, and held him up, shouting, "The future of Russia." He put the boy down and told him how Russia was going to change, that he would grow up in a new Russia, free of poverty and violence, where all people would be equal under God, and the law. He just couldn't seem to pull himself away in that moment. I looked around noticing the various buildings, the forest, it was all part of the moment. He walked back up to the platform with a certain glow, he had the feel of a saint. He spoke very confidently, "That was great, I wish we never had to leave," smiling, as he, Oleg, Kolya and I stood there, like we were on the highest mountain peak.

Then it happened.

A sharp crackle whizzed through the air. A flock of black birds flew into the sky. We instinctively looked towards Alexei. A puzzled look crossed over Alexei's handsome face, he looked down towards his stomach, putting his right hand over it. We didn't quite realize what was happening. I had never heard that sound before, what I now know is a rifle shot. Then another shot rang out, as Alexei grasped his chest and collapsed. The bullets had struck him in the back and went right through him. The guards looked around frantically, but no one was to be seen. They worked to hold back the crowd that was now shouting, sobbing, and wailing. I got down on the ground and pulled Alexei into my lap, as Oleg squatted grasping his hand. Kolya sat right next to me, looking like he wanted to pull Alexei from my hands. Alexei looked up his voice weak.

Alexei, "They finally got me. I will see you in heaven, my dear friends, Oleg, Kolya, Sergei, trust in God," then he was silent, as he bled out all over me. His beautiful blue eyes wide open, his mouth hung open, but even in that horror, there was a sense of serene peace on his still handsome face, as if his spirit had exited his body and went straight to heaven.

Oleg kept on repeating Alexei's name, "Alexei, Alexei, Alexei," as if somehow he would wake up, as if those bullets would go backwards out of his body, and back into the gun or guns from which they came, as tears came down his cheeks. Kolya sat there crying over Alexei's body. I just wailed and bawled like a three-year-old child, I had never cried like that in my life, I have never cried like that since. I think the guards thought I was possessed. Joy came running from the train, licking his master's face.

The guards' eyes were clearly watering, as if they wanted to cry with us, one of them gently informed us, "We need to take the Tsar back to Petrograd." But Oleg, Kolya and I wouldn't let go of Alexei's body, as if the guards didn't exist. If I could see the person who did this, I would have ripped them from limb to limb, but nothing, no one. It was as if a ghost had shot my kind, gentle, brave Alexei.

Chapter 12

Who murdered my dear sweet Alexei, it has become one of the enduring mysteries of our time. We know no more today than when I sat bawling on that platform with Alexei's lifeless body in my lap. But everyone wanted a piece of him, he was everything to everyone, they all claimed Alexei to be their hero. Those of us who were close to Alexei always believed that Lenin did it. Lenin's overture was just too convenient, for a man that had threatened and dismissed Alexei in life but was now embracing him in death. I wanted to shoot Lenin in the face. Lenin claimed the Monarchists did it, that "Comrade Alexei" was about ready to resign as Tsar and endorse their agenda. Some even claimed it was the Liberals fearing that Alexei was slipping from Kerensky's control.

The Kerensky government's last accomplishment was the shrine to Alexei. The Alexander Palace became a museum in his honor. He was buried out front with a huge bronze likeness over his grave. The train we traveled on was preserved, and plaques were erected at each spot in his now famous odyssey through Russia. The Monarchists moved against Kerensky in an attempted coup and then the Bolsheviks in a successful revolt, by November the Kerensky government was gone. If Kerensky had fled the Winter

Palace ten minutes later, he would have been killed. I remember that last day when Oleg came to get me. I insisted we take Kolya as well. We fled into exile with the Kerenskys, to New York. Alexander Kerensky expressed his deep regret that he couldn't save Alexei and lamented that if only Alexei had listened to him more, maybe things would have been different. Kerensky died a forgotten man.

Anti-Communist forces united under the White movement, to take back Russia from the Communists, throwing Russia into the Civil War Alexei had so feared, but the Whites ultimately failed. Tsar Nikolai and his family were evacuated by the British from Crimea. Alexandra in poor health was not long for this world, some say she died of a broken heart. Tsar Nikolai or so I have been told spent his final years in extreme sadness, puttering around in the garden, lamenting that he had failed Russia, and couldn't save his beloved son. Alexei's sisters, greatly saddened by Alexei's death, eventually married British nobility. Anastasia even wrote a book.

Lenin got his in the end, dying of a stroke not long after some woman shot him. But Lenin's prophetic vision came true, and Russia drowned in blood. After the Civil War, Stalin purged the country, and then there was World War II. But through it all, though the Communists downplayed "Comrade Alexei," they never attempted to dismantle his memory, and left his shrine intact.

The Communists fell and there is now a new hope through Russia. Alexei's memory is becoming more prominent again, as people work for Alexei's kind gentle vision for Russia. The Russian Orthodox Church even made him a saint, and people claim miracles at his grave. There are some who claim Alexei was the innocent sacrifice sent by God to atone for the sins of the Russian people.

Now it is August 12th, 1994, Alexei would be 90 years old today. I have been back in Russia for the first time since I fled. I visited the train we had ridden through the country on, and went up to the Alexander Palace, where Alexei and I spent our youth. They are untouched by time, looking just like we left them. The bedroom we slept in, Alexei's Island where we would swim out to the playhouse, it all came swirling back to me, as if time stood still. I was even mentioned in some of the placards as the friend whom Alexei spent his house arrest with. They sadly have his blood-stained uniform in the front entry way. Some have offered millions for it. The chess set in the bedroom is noted to be a duplicate of the original that disappeared. It will be returned in my will, I had to have something of his to remember him by.

I am now standing before Alexei's grave, staring at his statue, his handsome finely chiseled features in that simple army uniform he wore, but his giant bronze statue doesn't quite capture the young man I once knew, his beautiful blue eyes, his infectious laugh, his deep empathy, and incredible kindness, his fun-loving nature. I will be 90 years old soon, everyone from my youth except Kolya is dead, we are the last living memories of the real Alexei. I have come to see my Alexei one last time before I join him in heaven. I lived my life, but I never married, I never had kids, I couldn't find the ability to commit to another human being like I did to Alexei. Some say Alexei failed, some say it was all in vain, but I know they are wrong. Alexei achieved his goal, he brought hope to the Russian people, a hope that survived through all those terrible years of Russian history and survives to this day. Alexei, my friend, my brother, my Tsar, I love you. Sometimes you have to believe in miracles, sometimes you have to believe in God.

Author's Epilogue

This time we wanted history to be different, this time we wanted Alexei to live, and maybe save Russia. But alas, without a nod to the great man theory of history, it had to mostly return to its known course. In the end, Alexei could not overcome the waves of history that created the Russian Revolution. But what did Alexei do with the five years of extra life he was given in our alternative timeline? He may have indirectly saved his family, and he gave what he said the Russian people needed most, hope, becoming an enduring source of inspiration. Alexei did not make major changes to history, but he did bend it. His extra five years on this earth created ripples that are still felt today in our alternative timeline.

Bibliography

Special Thanks

Hawkins, George: *Alexei: Russia's Last Tsesarevich - Letters, diaries and writings.* 2022

Other Books

Buxhoeveden, Sophie: *The Life and Tragedy of Alexandra Feodorovna.* Longmans, Green and CO., 1928

Gilliard, Pierre: *Thirteen Years at the Russian Court.* Hutchinson & CO., 1921

Hanbury-Williams, John: *The Emperor Nicholas II, As I Knew Him.* Arthur L. Humphreys, 1922

Holy Trinity Publications: *The Romanovs Under House Arrest: From the 1917 Diary of a Palace Priest.* 2018

Massie, Robert K: *Nicholas and Alexandra.* Atheneum, 1967

Mesa Potamos Publications: *The Romanov Royal Martyrs: What Silence Could Not Conceal.* 2023

Vyrubova, Anna: *Memories of the Russian Court.* Macmillan & CO., 1923